McDragon

McDRAGON

PAM G HOWARD

Matador
9 Priory Business Park,
Wistow Road, Kibworth Beauchamp,
Leicestershire. LE8 0RX
Tel: 0116 279 2299
Email: books@troubador.co.uk
Web: www.troubador.co.uk/matador
Twitter: @matadorbooks

ISBN 978 1788032 643

British Library Cataloguing in Publication Data.
A catalogue record for this book is available from the British Library.

Printed and bound by CPI Group (UK) Ltd, Croydon, CR0 4YY
Typeset in 11pt Minion Pro by Troubador Publishing Ltd, Leicester, UK

Matador is an imprint of Troubador Publishing Ltd

For Fin

BOOKS BY PAM G HOWARD

The McDragon series
McDragon

Mr Spangle series
Spangle

CHAPTER ONE

The dragon snorted as he slumbered, warming the rocks in front of him. He was dreaming about a boy, but not just any boy, he was picturing the one who dragon lore foretold might find that which had been stolen from them.

* * *

He could see them waiting for him the other side of the school gates and Peter hesitated before he crossed the road, then he dropped his gaze downwards at the pavement and scurried forward as quickly as he could. Why on earth had he mentioned dragons in class yesterday? Just because he hadn't been paying attention he had said the first thing that had come into his head. He looked up briefly and saw some children near the main entrance point at him and snigger and then he heard the scuffling of feet near him and got a waft of bad breath and sweaty armpits. The dreaded voice spoke against his left ear.

"Nice to see you Dragon Boy! Dragons, I ask you… what world do you live in Crip?!" and an elbow jabbed him painfully in the side pushing him hard against the wall. There was a nasty laugh as the voice threatened quietly, "We'll catch up with you later! Have to make the most of the last day at school! Where are you going on holiday… Southend again for the day?"

"Actually, we are going to a villa in Spain!" Peter blurted out hoping his nose wouldn't grow with the lie.

Biffy looked at him disbelievingly and gave him another shove in the ribs as he sauntered off down the corridor chortling to himself about dragons as he did.

Peter pushed himself off the wall and then plodded on towards his classroom. The school day always started the same way no matter what he did and he was sure that as it went on it was going to get far, far, worse.

He remembered the conversation with his mum that morning when she'd said they were going by car to Scotland for the summer holidays.

"Why do we have to go somewhere like that? Everyone else goes to Spain and Turkey or somewhere in an aeroplane!"

Mum looked at him quietly, "Dad has to go there with his work and we're lucky that we are all able to go with him. The alternative would mean we have to stay at home throughout the summer."

His face fell. He could just picture Biffy Jones' face when he heard that "The Crip" as they nicknamed him was not going to a sunny fun place like everyone else. The Crip, so named because he had a hand with only two fingers and a thumb on it.

Apparently, the Isle of Harris was in the Outer Hebrides in Scotland and everyone knew that it rained there all of the time. Biffy was going to have a field day with him when he found out and as he'd trudged to school in the drizzle he made his mind up; he was not going to tell anyone where he was going on holiday.

When the bell went for lunch he dawdled and let everyone get out before him so that he could scan the playground and check where Biffy and his mates were. He clocked them giving little Steven Parker a hard time and nipped around the corner quickly in the hope he could eat his lunch undisturbed for once.

He gave a small shudder as he got the whiff of sweat nearby and, before he could move, he heard feet on the tarmac and realised that Biffy had crept up beside him. Biffy swung his arm out and knocked the sandwich box to the ground. White sliced bread with cheese and pickle oozed out from under Biffy's foot as he purposefully wriggled it from side to side.

"Oops! Sorry!" he smirked.

Peter froze, he knew better than to move a muscle.

"Rhonda spoke to your sister and it seems you are a liar. Not only are you a crippled idiot to believe in dragons but a liar as well to boot! Liar liar pants on fire!" the voice crowed in his ear, bad breath accompanying it. "This is what happens to liars!" Bully boy Biffy pulled a lighter out of his pocket. Rhonda was Biffy's sister and she was in the same class as Alice, Peter's sister.

"You're not allowed th..that!" Peter stuttered.

"Who's going to stop me Crip? You? This is what'll teach you to lie to me! We don't like liars do we boys?"

There was a murmur of agreement and then the lighter flicked and the inevitable small yellow and blue

3

flame sprang up. Peter tried to move away but he was surrounded by the smirking group of five boys. The flame touched the back of his trousers and he could smell the material singeing and then the pain of a burn. It hurt. He gritted his teeth trying not to yell out.

"As I said, liar, liar pants on fire! Let that be a lesson to you Dragon Boy not to tell me lies! A poor boy like you couldn't go to Spain where the sun shines! You're going to Scotland where it rains all the time!" Biffy almost cackled as he said it. "Now, say sorry for telling lies!"

Peter fought back the tears and murmured, "Sorry Biffy."

"Louder!"

"Sorry Biffy," he shouted.

"What are you doing over there lads?" called a teacher on lunch duty.

"Nothing, Miss!"

Peter breathed a big sigh of relief as the gang moved away from him. He gingerly felt through the hole in the back of his trousers where the burn was raw on his leg. His mum was going to kill him when he got home!

He picked up his lunch box and looked hopefully at the bread on the ground. All that was left was a slimy mess of squashed cheese and brown pickle. He was going to be hungry… again.

CHAPTER TWO

There was one particular part of the long boring journey up the motorway to Scotland that Peter would always remember – the smell after Alice threw up out the window before his dad could pull over in time.

"Why is there always carrot and tomato skin in it?" he asked. His dad glared at him but didn't bother to reply, they were too busy trying to mop up the stray bits of sick which had blown back in through the window. The smell took a long time to go away.

The weather seemed to change as they crossed the Scottish border, from sunshine to rain and Peter peered gloomily out of the window in the dusk.

The movement of the car rocked him gently and his eyelids gradually fluttered down as his head nodded, his chin resting on his chest.

He woke as he felt the car slow to a halt. They had made a couple of stops on the way so his dad and mum could have a nap and change drivers and they could also eat some squishy smelly egg sandwiches which someone had sat on, so they were very flat.

It was a great relief to everyone when they finally reached Uig where they were catching the ferry to Tarbert.

"You can get out and have a look about but don't go far. Come back once you see the ferry come into the harbour."

"And stay together and keep away from the edge!" added mum as they scrambled out of the car to hare across the quayside.

"Look, Peter, what's that looking at us?"

As he peered into the sea where Alice was pointing a head slipped back down under the surface. A moment later the sleek black head reappeared.

"Ohh, it's a seal! Look there is another one!" and they happily spent their time trying to count the seals bobbing their heads up and down in front of them like a puppet show.

"Ten!" shouted Peter triumphantly, "I've never seen a seal before except at the zoo!"

Big seagulls shrieked noisily in the air landing on the jetty, squabbling every now and then over scraps of food they found on the dock. They looked very big and fierce with their long yellow beaks. The seals took no notice of them as they carried on their examination of the children from the safety of the water.

A shout summoned them back to the car and it wasn't long before they were standing on deck watching Uig disappear into the distance.

"Bye bye seals," cried Alice.

They had fish and chips on the ferry and, naturally, Alice was sick again.

"When we go mackerel fishing we won't need to take any bait," said dad dryly to Peter. "We can just feed Alice and let her be sick over the side of the boat. That'll attract the fish!"

"Do fish like tomato skins?" enquired Peter and his dad just grunted in amusement.

"Will we get to keep the fish we catch?"

"Yes, fresh fish that you catch yourself is always much tastier than anything you buy."

"I don't think I fancy eating a fish that's full of Alice's sick!"

"I was joking lad! We actually don't need to take bait with us anyway as the fish chase the shiny lures that are tied onto the lines and then get hooked up when you move the fishing line upwards. You'll see."

Peter was very relieved at that.

The car rolled off the ferry at Tarbert amidst the shouts of the seamen directing them. They stopped to pick up some supplies in the small shops in the village and then set off the short distance to the small house that dad's firm had rented for them for the summer.

Peter looked about him, it was a totally different landscape to what they had been used to. Shaggy sheep could be heard bahing and he could see them dotted about on the grassy areas, some trailing wool that made them look like a bride with a long train.

"Dad, why do the sheep all look like someone has painted splodges on them?"

"That's how the crofters know which sheep belong to which croft. The smaller sheep are this year's lambs." he said slowing down to avoid a ewe ambling across the road in front of them. Another just lay peacefully in the kerbside chewing contentedly with a lamb tucked safely into her side.

At long last they pulled into the driveway of a little white walled house.

Almost before the car had stopped Peter flung himself out of the door.

"Not so fast young man, we have work to do first. The white house is not where we are staying, they just let us park our car here. We have to carry all of our luggage a few hundred yards around the corner, along that track over there," and he pointed to where they could just see a roof showing above the small hillside, a rough stony track leading to it.

The next half hour was tortuous as far as Peter was concerned. They each had to carry their luggage along the track at the top of the small cliffs and leave it by the house. Then they had to tramp back to the car and help with the other goods they had brought with them, and hump them along the uneven track. By his second trip Peter was puffing with the effort of carrying the heavy packages and was very relieved to see his mum signalling at the open front door to let him know that he could come in.

Dad told him where his luggage should go and left it to Peter to heave both his and Alice's cases, one at a time, up to their rooms. He dumped Alice's on her bed and then checked out his own room. It was very small with just a single bed, a wardrobe and a chest of drawers but he felt it was the nicest bedroom because his window looked down onto the little beach. He threw his belongings into the wardrobe and drawers and thumped down the stairs to find his mum cutting up a cake she had bought to go with a cup of tea.

"Can I eat mine by the sea?"

"Yes, but stay in sight of the house please."

He scampered along to the tiny beach, across the stones and pebbles and stood by the water's edge and took in a deep breath. It smelt amazing here, so very different to what he was used to.

"No Biffy either!" he thought contentedly.

He stopped to take a bite out of his cake and listened. There was a peep peep noise over by the rocks on the beach and he saw a couple of black and white birds with long thin red beaks take off and fly low across the water to the rocks on the other side of the beach. It was, well, just peaceful with only the sound of the water lapping on the shore and the birds communicating with one another.

CHAPTER THREE

Next morning saw him up at the crack of dawn eager to be outside despite the late night. It seemed because they were so far north the darkness of the night didn't start until about eleven o'clock and then the sun rose very early in the morning. Peter crept out of the small box room and down the stairs, stopping in the kitchen only to grab an apple and then he was out, running free. It was a wonderful feeling – all he could hear was the peep peeping of the birds that his dad had said were oyster catchers. Another slight splashing sound caught his attention and he turned. An otter was lying on its back in the sea only a few yards in front of him eating a big fish! Luckily, he had his little camera with him and he grabbed it out of his pocket and snapped and snapped. Beautiful. He was transfixed as it finished its snack and dived down to come up with yet another shiny fish.

"Wow!"

The clouds chased one another across the sky over the rocks to the left of the tiny beach. Because the tide was out he could see different lines of colour on the rocks. There was the green kelp which he knew from his nature books that the otters liked, and then the black rock topped off with grass and more rocks with bright yellow lichen on them. He focussed the camera and clicked away.

The otter had moved on round to the next bay so he crunched his way across the pebbles to go exploring.

As he got closer to the rocky peninsular he looked at the outline of it with the sun shining behind it. "It looks like a lizard... no, that's not right I think it's a sleeping dragon!"

Peter felt it was his duty to go and investigate the so called dragon. The rocks which shaped it were deep black with yellow speckled lichen running from what Peter imagined would be the highest point on the dragon's head down its long spiny neck.

He started to crunch across the little beach towards it, checking all the time where to put each of his wellie booted feet. It was very slippery in places where the rocks were shrouded in seaweed. His foot slithered on a piece of mushy green kelp and before he knew it, he'd landed in a heap with his face just touching the water in a small pool. The knees of his jeans were wet and grubby but other than that he was fine. As his eyes focussed on the pool he saw a crab scuttling off sideways when it spotted the large shadow looming over it, its pincers where waving threateningly above its head as it moved.

He was transfixed for a moment watching black sea snails creeping slowly across the rocks under the water and then a small starfish lying peacefully at the bottom of the pool

His tummy rumbled.

Picking himself up and brushing any bits of rock and sand off his trousers he went as quickly as he could across the beach towards the house. Exploring was completely forgotten as the smell of bacon wafted past his nose and he heard the chatter of voices coming from the little cottage.

He stopped near the doorway and looked back.

"Don't worry Mr Dragon I will be visiting you soon!"

"There you are son. Hungry?" and his mum thrust a bacon buttie into his hand almost as soon as he had burst through the front door and settled his bottom on a kitchen chair. It was pushed hungrily into his mouth as spluttering through it he said, "I've been exploring. I saw a crab, and a starfish and sea snails…" crumbs spat from his mouth and he drew in a big breath "and an otter eating fish and… what did you say those birds were that go "peep peep" dad?"

"Don't speak with your mouth full Peter!"

"Sorry mum." He swallowed and then repeated his question about the birds.

"Oyster catchers. You didn't go very far did you?"

"No just on the beach. I think there is a dragon sitting on the rocks over there!"

Alice laughed, "Don't be silly, there aren't such things as dragons! You made everyone at school laugh when you mentioned them!"

"Well, it could be one!" he said petulantly.

Peter looked over his shoulder. He felt his "dragon" almost pulling his gaze there.

"Tomorrow," he whispered, "Tomorrow I will come and see you!"

After breakfast they all had a wonderful time beachcombing in the nearby bay. Peter even found a couple of oysters which he proudly handed to his dad saying, "Hide those from the oyster catchers dad!" It had been worth getting a boot full of water trying to reach them.

For once there were no arguments about bed – being an explorer was a tiring business.

* * *

The next morning Peter couldn't wait to get out of bed, which was unusual, normally he just wanted to hide under the covers, putting off the moment when he had to go to school and face Biffy the bully. Again, he grabbed an apple as he passed the fruit bowl, this time saying, "An apple a day keeps the doctor away! Mum will be pleased."

He found his wellington boots upside down outside on the broom and mop handles where they had dried out perfectly and then he was off – picking his way as fast as he could towards his black and yellow dragon rock.

There was no sign of the otter today.

He scrambled up the rock, his hands getting a little scratched on the rough black rocks and finally arrived puffing and panting next to where he imagined the big dragon head to be.

"You certainly look like a dragon to me!" he announced happily. He looked along the top of the rocks down what would have been the spines on a long neck until the black rocks widened out into a body and finally narrowed down to look almost like a tail. There was even a ridge each side where he could pretend that huge wings were folded up.

He put out his left hand, the one with only one thumb and two fingers, and touched the top rock very gently. The rocks were warm to touch, which seemed strange as the sun had not risen in the sky enough to warm them. They looked different closer to, the yellow appearing more like golden sparkles. He tentatively stroked his hand over the top rock again, "Hello Mr Dragon!"

He smiled as he straddled where the neck joined the body and pictured himself soaring over the sea with the wind bustling at him and the dragon roaring in delight to have found a new friend.

"I have always wanted to ride a dragon! You must be a McDragon as we are in Scotland!"

He toppled off of his seat and bounced down the side of the rocks as a big voice boomed through his head, "You are correct! I am McDragon and you are Petersmith!"

"Y..you know me?"

"I've been waiting for you," was the response.

"For me? How could you possibly know about me?"

"I will explain all in good time Petersmith."

The rock which he was touching gently moved beneath his hand and Peter's mouth opened in a large O shape as he took in a deep breath.

"Are… are you a real dragon?"

"Of course! I am one of the oldest inhabitants on Harris and very few humans who are alive have ever seen me."

Peter stared in amazement at the rocks which looked like they were melting away changing into something else, something truly magnificent. A dragon!

"Where are your wings?"

"Patience lad, you will soon see. It takes a little while

for me to wake my body up after such a long time." said the deep powerful voice in his head.

"This can't be true," muttered Peter pinching himself.

The dragon shrugged and his whole body rippled as he grew. He was the size of a small plane and his wings when they unfolded were the same length as his whole head, body and tail. Coal black scales of differing sizes, like a jigsaw, fitted neatly down the whole of him with gold spattered all along his back and neck. He stretched out his wings away from his body and they moved gracefully up and down. Peter felt the air displaced by them nearly blowing him backwards into the sea.

The neck arched as McDragon bent round to bring his enormous face up closer to Peter's.

Amethyst eyes looked straight into Peter's face. For some reason he felt no fear.

"I am talking to a real dragon! Wow. Can I take a picture of you please?" and he brandished his camera in McDragon's face.

The lens snapped a couple of times and then Peter pushed the camera safely down into the bottom of his pocket to make sure he didn't lose it.

"I knew you would come Petersmith."

"How?"

"It was foretold."

"What do you mean?"

"Petersmith, it was said you would be the one to find what has been stolen. I can show you if you are brave enough to fly with me?"

Peter looked amazed, "You can fly and I can r..ride on your back?"

"Would you like to?"

"I th..think so!" he stammered.

"But how on earth can I be the one to find what has been stolen? I cannot fly, I cannot even drive. I do swim fairly well though." He announced. "What is it anyway that you have lost?"

"Seraphina's Pearl – something very rare in our dragon lives now. We have searched high and low for it but there is no trace. Seraphina was desolate when it was stolen and went into a deep decline. She nearly turned white until it was foretold that Petersmith would come and return it to us. Now her colour is returning bit by bit and she will be so delighted that you have finally arrived after waiting all this time."

"Well, I am happy to help you but I will need to let my mum and dad know."

"You cannot tell a soul, Petersmith!" roared the dragon in his head.

"But I can't just go off on a hunt for Seraphina's Pearl, whatever that might be, without telling them."

"They wouldn't understand or believe you. But do not worry, dragon time is different to human time. I can take you now to see where it is written. It will be in dragon time and I can bring you back for your breakfast today in human time, which means your family will be none the wiser. Trust me!"

"Breakfast today?"

"Definitely!" was the firm answer. "Once I have shown you the future and some of the past, you can go back to your house and then think about whether you will help. I will not force you because that is not the dragon way."

16

"Hmm, I need to think a moment. I am not allowed to go with strangers but no-one has ever said anything about going with a dragon!"

"We are in dragon time now so you do not need to rush to decide."

"Where do we have to go?"

"Up there," and McDragon flicked his tail towards the distant mountains. "Higher than where the eagles go."

"No-one will believe I have flown with a dragon! Yes, I will come with you, but you have to promise that I will be back for breakfast. Anyway, you wouldn't want to be with me if I get hungry because I get very bad tempered!"

McDragon gave what must have been a dragon smile as his eyes went from amethyst to gold. He nodded majestically at the boy before him.

"A dragon's word is sacred. We have made our agreement." And his eyes returned to their normal amethyst colour. "Now, climb up onto my back where you were before I awoke. Hold very tight to my crest. I will close down my scales onto your legs to keep you firmly attached to me so you do not fall." he commanded.

CHAPTER FOUR

It was not so easy climbing onto a live dragon's back with one disabled hand and he was also feeling a bit bruised from his fall after McDragon had first spoken to him. What made it even more difficult was that the sleek black scales were shiny and hard. In the end McDragon had to push Peter's bottom with his snout to get him into the right position. Peter wriggled his backside backwards and forwards until he was relatively comfortable, seated between two upright spines at the base of the neck and beginning of the body. He felt dragon scales close down over his thin legs. These were surprisingly soft and warm underneath and he felt very secure.

"Ready!"

The wide wings whooshed quietly up and down slowly at first and then gradually gathering speed as the great dragon's body lifted straight up into the air. They were off!

"Whoopee!" screamed Peter as he felt them glide through the air. It was getting colder the higher they went and he started to shiver. The dragon turned to check he was alright and then flew swiftly, higher and higher, over the locks and burns and fern and bracken covered hills. The houses seemed like tiny matchboxes and anyone looking up would just think they were a big bird.

Peter stared along McDragon's long neck and could see that they were headed towards a long low cave mouth with a black opening very high up in the mountain. Far below them were two eagles ducking and diving looking down on the ground from a great height for their dinner.

"You may need to hold on very tightly, Petersmith, I am not that practised at landing here!" and Peter ducked down as he could see the entrance of the cave coming towards them at a very fast rate of knots. There was a loud thump thump as McDragon's talons touched the ledge, and then he carried on pounding into the cave. His wings knocked out some rocks at the sides of the walls as he entered.

"Oops, sorry, I forgot I needed to slow down a little on landing!"

They juddered to a halt some way into the cavern.

"You can get down now." puffed the dragon.

Peter felt the scales release his legs and he slipped down the shiny side of the dragon, shivering as he did and wrapping his arms around him.

The dragon looked down at him and realised how cold the small boy was.

"Don't move from that spot!" he growled and drew in a deep breath, fire rushing out of his nostrils onto the sides of the cavern as he moved his head slowly from side to side until the rocks around them glowed red.

Peter immediately felt warmer, in fact, so much so he was almost too hot.

"Oh dear, look at the tips of your wings!"

Black dragon blood was oozing out of the gashes from where they had crashed into the rocks at the side of the cave's entrance.

"Hmm, nothing a little dragon spit will not fix." Peter ducked very quickly as a large dragon wing brushed over his head and then McDragon spat and green globules covered the end of the wing. There was a hissing sound and the wounds healed up. All that remained was the smell of something like very burnt toast.

Peter's tummy rumbled and the dragon tipped his head to the side as he heard it.

"Ok! Ok!" he grumbled, "I know you need to get back to break your fast. Your tummy doesn't seem to understand dragon time! Follow me!" and he spun round, quite elegantly for such a big being. Peter had to duck yet again to miss being sideswiped by that long strong tail.

He trotted obediently after the dragon. "How will we see?"

"Well, when I warmed you it also made the tunnel glow all the way through the mountain."

"Are we walking all that way… right to the other side?"

"No Petersmith, that would take far too long for a human boy who is hungry."

As he jogged along Peter stared at the sides of the huge tunnel they were moving through, making sure that he also kept an eye on where McDragon was. He didn't want to be left here on his own.

"Not that I can get down by myself!" he thought as he realised that he was quite reliant on the dragon keeping his promise and taking him back to his mum and dad.

He might possibly have been quite foolish. How could he know he could trust McDragon? He might be trapped here forever!

The sides of the tunnel were very smooth and pale grey. Every few yards a warm glow came from one of the walls giving out light and warmth.

Peter suddenly banged into the end of the dragon's tail.

"Ow! That hurt!" It was like walking into a sharp rock.

McDragon bent his big head around and peered down at the boy.

"Look where you are going then. I will not be able to heal you the way I could my wings."

Then he pointed with his snout at the wall beside him. There were etchings engraved into the smooth rock.

"This depicts the beginning of the world of dragons. See the two magicians, each in their tower?" McDragon said as he touched the wall with his nose. "See also the stone dragons on the top of the walls Petersmith?" Peter nodded it was like a story in pictures.

Sparks were shooting out of one of the magician's wands into the air meeting with a coloured burst of light from the other magician who was dressed in purple. He had a big pointy purple hat on, just like a magician should. Both magicians had long beards, again just like wizards should have. The next picture showed the magician who was dressed in purple had turned and pointed his wand towards the highest point of his tower. Behind him the stone dragons that had been decorating the top of the tower could be seen coming alive and flying down towards the black clothed magician, wings outstretched and breathing fire. They looked truly ferocious.

The magician in black retaliated and gargoyles which had been lining the path to his tower sprung up. They could not stand up straight and were hunched over. They all had long fingernails, the same length as their hands, and they pointed with these at the dragons as they charged at them.

The next sketch had the magicians with their backs towards one another and in the following picture they were both gone in a puff of smoke.

"Those were the two magicians who started our lives, Murani, the one in purple and Lukan in black. None of us dragons know to this day if they survived the battle or not or even what they were fighting about, but fight they did and it was a very violent one. However, as you now know the dragons did survive and breed. Sadly, our numbers are rather depleted but there are a few dragons remaining spread over Scotland. Others can be found in different countries in your world, generally unseen by human beings, although I believe there are various myths told about them."

"What about the gargoyles?"

"They still exist. They have evolved into something much more deadly. Squawkins. They are now a red colour and if you ever see one be very aware of their long pointed nails, a scratch from one of them could mean death to a human. Let's move on to the end."

He carried on past many, many drawings until they finally came to the penultimate picture.

"See here," McDragon said in his deep voice in Peter's head and Peter looked. His eyes opened very wide in surprise and his mouth formed a big "O". There was the picture of a very black dragon with gold splashed along his back and amethyst eyes. Beside him a small thin boy, with mousey brown hair and a box that looked much like a camera, dressed exactly as Peter was today in jeans and a blue jumper. Then, even more amazing was the fact it showed he was missing two fingers on his left hand. Etched next to him was the name, "Petersmith".

McDragon hurried him to another drawing where Peter was being touched on his forehead by a shiny pale sea blue dragon, speckled with grey. McDragon was beside Peter and both dragons somehow looked happy.

"That is Seraphina." McDragon announced.

CHAPTER FIVE

Peter was incredibly hungry when he flung open the door of the cottage. There was no-one there! He panicked, perhaps dragontime didn't really exist. Maybe his parents were out searching for him!

He heard the chain pulling in the bathroom and a sigh of relief went through him. His mum's slippers on the stairs were the first thing he saw, and he ran over to her to give her a big hug.

"What's this for? Are you hungry?"

"Oh yes, I've been up exploring for ages!"

"Put the kettle on then please Peter."

He did as he was told and got the cups out to make the tea.

"What is that?" he asked. She was cutting thick slices from a long sausage roll. Another one sat on the chopping board beside it.

"This is Scottish black pudding and that one is Scottish white pudding. We are going to have a slice of each with fried egg. It is good to try some local food while we are here."

"What is it made of? Is it like pork sausage?"

"No, nothing like that but I think you will like it. Best not to know what is in it before you eat it."

They could hear dad's heavy footsteps coming down the stairs making some of them creak and then he came into the kitchen and peered into the frying pan.

"Oooh, lovely! Black pudding and fried egg. Oh, Peter, good news. I don't have to work today after all so this afternoon we could go fishing if you like. We'll need to go into Tarbert to get some fishing equipment. Does that appeal to you?"

"Yes please!"

"I'll give Callum a ring and see if he can take us out in his boat."

Both Alice and Peter enjoyed the black pudding, especially with the egg and lots of tomato sauce on it. They followed this down with toast and marmalade. After washing up they went down to the little beach to see how far the tide had gone out, while dad made arrangements for the fishing.

Peter looked across at McDragon's rocks as he walked along and thought about his adventure that morning. What should he do? On their flight back the dragon had told him that the loss of Seraphina's Pearl could be the start of the dragons fading out and becoming extinct. That was a big thing to take onto his young shoulders. They would be like dodos and it could be his fault. What McDragon hadn't explained though was exactly what Seraphina's Pearl was.

Alice called to him and that brought him out of his reverie and he went to stare into the rock pool she had found. There was a small crab in it which hid when Peter's shadow crossed the pool. There were more of the small black water snails and lots of barnacles clinging to one of the rocks.

Peter put his hand into the water and brought one of the snails up. It immediately disappeared into its shell so he tossed it back in.

"Peter! Do you still want to come with me to the general store to get our fishing supplies?" dad shouted across the beach.

"Yes please! I'm coming now!" and he raced back towards the house, leaping over the rocky pools.

"Careful, don't rush in case you trip!"

Peter was fascinated by the shop when they arrived, it was nothing like the DIY stores where they lived, everything was crammed in different corners in a jumble in the dark building, pots of paint, brushes, brooms, buckets, hooks, ropes. It was like an Aladdin's cave but for builders and fisherman.

"Ah yes, these are what we want!" Dad pushed his hand deep into a box and came out with four darrows, which were plastic rectangular frames that had fishing line wound round them. He also bought four lead weights, because as he explained, the weights on the darrows were not heavy enough to take the lines deep enough. He added some coloured feathers and also some black ones to his purchases saying that these would be tied onto the fishing line to tempt the fish to close their mouths onto the hooks.

"These will be fine for catching mackerel. We are not here long enough to warrant getting any fishing rods."

In no time at all they were back at the house. Dad put

the new weights and feathers onto each darrow, showing Peter the special fisherman's knot needed to secure them. Peter found out how sharp the hooks were when one embedded itself in his finger and dad had to carefully ease it out. Each hook had the feathers on them which glittered in the sun. Apparently the fish would think these were small fish flashing in the water and, surprisingly, the black feathers would work just as well under the water.

After a quick bite to eat they drove around to the other side of the bay to the small quayside that had been built specially for launching boats, stopping to pick up Alice and his mum on the way. Callum was waiting for them in a small boat. Peter was told that the small covered area at the front, or bow of the boat was called a cuddy and it had seats inside however there were seats at the back as well and also a bench for the "captain" and his "mate".

Peter was so excited that all thoughts of dragons were very far from his mind as he hopped into the boat. It rocked from side to side as he settled himself down on a seat at the stern of the boat. Alice followed shortly behind him and mum sat in the cuddy. Callum fired up the engine and they zoomed across the bay, spray splashing their faces as they did. It was exhilarating.

Peter and Alice were each wearing brightly coloured life jackets. "Just in case." His mum had said as they were zipped into them. His parents wore life jackets too.

It took about half an hour but finally the engine slowed.

"Mid sound rock is beneath us now and it can be a good place to catch fish. We'll try here until we drift too close to the shore." Callum told them in his thick Scottish accent as he cut the engine.

Dad handed the darrows out, warning them all to be very careful of the hooks. Peter nodded, looking at the plaster which was wrapped around one of his fingers after his experience earlier in the day with the hook.

They all unwound the lines slowly into the water and then gave them gentle tugs to move the lures through the water. Callum smiled as he watched them.

"Dad, I felt something like a little nudge on my line!" shouted Peter importantly.

"Reel her in very quickly then laddie!"

Peter wound his line round and round the darrow as fast as he could. The line was feeling heavier and heavier and jerking, but he knew the end of it was in sight when he saw silver flashes through the dark water getting closer and closer to the boat.

Callum pulled a bucket across the floor of the boat and as the fish tumbled over the side he grabbed each one of the slippery wriggling fish and knocked them on the head with what Peter decided was a "bonker" and then took the hooks gently out of their mouths. They looked beautiful, silver and blue and sleek sitting in the bottom of the bucket. The bonk on the head had killed them so they could not feel anything.

"Six! I caught six!" he shouted excitedly.

Suddenly Alice called out and her catch was landed the same way. Mum and dad also had fish on their lines so it was mayhem in the small boat for quite a time.

"Must have been lucky and hit a shoal," Callum said smilingly as he despatched each fish into the bucket.

Eventually, the contented fisherfolk returned home satisfied with their afternoon's work. As they had caught so many fish between them they left quite a few with Callum. Mum decided that for dinner tonight they would have grilled mackerel with mashed potato and maybe cabbage mixed with fried onion, which they all liked. There would be some horseradish sauce as well because this seemed to go nicely with mackerel.

"I've had such fun today," said Peter tiredly as he kissed each of his parents goodnight after dinner, and as soon as his head touched the pillow he was off into a deep sleep where he dreamed of dragons.

CHAPTER SIX

It was the rain pitter pattering on the window which woke
Peter. He stretched and snuggled further down under
the quilt. It was cosy there, but no matter how he tried,
sleep would not come back, so he lay there pondering on
the problem of the dragons and the quest for Seraphina's
Pearl. He still didn't know what the Pearl was – when he
had asked McDragon the answer had been, "Well, it's the
Pearl!"

The etchings hadn't shown just what Seraphina's Pearl
looked like either, so how was he to find it? Why did the
dragon seer who created the drawings with dragon magic
think he was the one who should be the seeker? What
made him special? Biffy and his gang didn't think he was
special – they just thought of him as a cripple.

So many questions.

He thought long and hard on the problem, then
realised it was quiet outside. He peeked through the
window and looked over the beach. McDragon was in his
rocky form silhouetted in the dawn light.

Perhaps they could fly again. He was sure it was more

exciting than being on a plane, not that he'd been on one but he had heard some of the other children talking about it.

He hopped out of bed and scooted quickly into the bathroom to have a wash. Mum insisted they washed and brushed their teeth before dressing. Feeling he had obeyed mum's rules, he slipped quietly down the stairs, grabbing an apple and then was straight out of the door. Then he stopped in his tracks… maybe it was all a dream.

The otter was having his breakfast on the left hand side of the bay but Peter decided to leave him in peace and continued across to the right where the dragon stones were highlighted by the rising sun.

The deep voice boomed inside of his head as he scrambled over the slippery rocks, "I hoped you would come today."

"Oh, it really did happen then?"

"Oh yes, Petersmith, most definitely."

Peter was transfixed as the rocks started to melt away as before eventually turning into the fabulous dragon. The head appeared first, large and fierce, then the long neck followed by the big body and legs with talons on the end and finally the lengthy powerful black tail. The spines along the back and tail were the last to straighten up and the black and yellow dragon stood before him.

"Let me take you to meet an old friend of mine."

Peter's eyes rounded and he smiled, "Flying?"

The dragon nodded his big head. "Yes, but it is a very long journey so before you come aboard wait and I will warm you," and heat rather than fire blew out of McDragon's nostrils warming Peter's body right down to his toes.

"Now, come on up. The heat will last for the length of the journey."

As previously, McDragon gave him a prod with his snout to aid Peter as he slithered his way up onto his back and settled himself down. It was tricky getting a good grip with a hand that had only one thumb and two fingers. The scales lifted around his knees and pressed down to clamp him securely onto his perch. The powerful enormous wings rose and fell, pulsing air around them as they lifted up and flew straight across the bay away from the house. Peter could see the salmon pens that they had passed when they had gone out on the boat. The water looked calm.

A variety of small green islands passed quickly beneath them, some with houses on them and then eventually they passed a town and harbour. McDragon stayed lower than he had the day before so that Peter could see everything.

"That is Uig beneath us now."

"We caught the ferry from there, but I can't see any seals from this high up."

"No, they would keep clear of me anyway, as they can be quite tasty to eat."

Peter blanched at the thought. Eventually he nodded off – it seemed like a very long journey.

When he woke up he could see and feel the wings gracefully moving at a steady pace and the land whizzing by beneath them. They flew over more sea and mountains and finally McDragon began a low dive.

"We are over the mainland now." But for all that it was still quite a while before Peter's ears popped as they began their descent down over a long black loch.

"This is Loch Ness." McDragon told him, and then

he performed a very rough and bouncy landing on some ground next to the loch and at the same time raising his snout into the air to emit a large hum which echoed around the loch.

"Watch the water in front of us," he said.

A big green head emerged from the blackness and a responding hum reverberated around them.

Peter watched in awe as another enormous dragon clambered out of the water. Streams of water cascaded down from him pouring back into the loch.

"This is Haribald d'Ness!"

"Very pleased to meet you." responded Peter politely.

"And Haribald, this is Petersmith!"

Haribald inclined his head towards Peter.

"Petersmith! At last! We have been waiting for your arrival for a long time." His voice echoed around Peter's head in greeting.

"Humans believe that Haribald is a monster called Nessie that lives in the loch and they are partly correct in that, but he is a dragon, not a monster. Humans cannot see a dragon unless that dragon wishes them to, so you are honoured, Petersmith." McDragon gave a little dragon chuckle as he said this.

Peter smiled at that. He wished that Biffy could see him now! Fancy Peter Smith, the Crip as they called him, being spoken to by two dragons! So much for laughing at him, it was nice to be right for once.

"I hope you decide to help us dragons," boomed Haribald, "because unless the Pearl is found, in time our kind could be doomed."

"But why me?"

"Because it has been written!"

"Can I say something please?"

Both dragons nodded in tandem.

"I know nothing about where to look for this Pearl, or how big it is or even what it looks like or … anything!" he exclaimed.

"You will overcome that lack of knowledge, have no fear. We have been searching for the Pearl for some years but it seems that only Petersmith will find it. I will be there to help you and you will, of course, be using dragontime."

"How did the Pearl get stolen?"

Haribald d'Ness looked very sad, if he had been human his shoulders would have drooped and he had a hangdog look about him.

"Seraphina was looking after the Pearl but had to go and hunt for food so she hid it in a very special place that only she and I knew. Someone must have been spying on her and then stole it while she was away. Seraphina was my dragonmate but after the Pearl was lost she was so heartbroken that she hid herself with magic somewhere and I have not seen her for a long time. Once she hears that Petersmith is finally here I am sure that Seraphina will return to us."

It was like a penny dropping in Peter's mind and smiling he announced loudly, "At last I understand! The Pearl is a dragon's egg!"

"Well you could put it like that I suppose… but it is a dragon's Pearl. That is what we call it."

"But what does it look like?"

"You would see it as a big speckled stone."

"OK then, what colour?" Peter could not believe getting the answers to the questions could be so hard.

"Well, it was like a smooth oval rock – the same colour as me but speckled with Seraphina's blue but as the dragonite inside the Pearl matures it changes to the colour of the dragon inside it."

Peter's stomach took that opportunity to rumble, it had been empty for some time.

"We must go Petersmith, your stomach still does not understand dragontime."

Haribald looked at Peter earnestly, "Our world and my happiness rests on your shoulders Petersmith, so I do hope you can see your way to help us. It would mean the world to me to see my Seraphina again and our Pearl. Goodbye for now," and the big dragon turned away with his head hanging low and waded back into the beautiful depths of Loch Ness until he was totally submerged and had disappeared from sight.

McDragon, true to his word, took Peter safely back to the house on Harris. Peter slept for a lot of the journey, after all he had left when it was dawn. As Peter turned to run back to the cottage McDragon said, "You have much to ponder on Petersmith, but remember the choice is yours as to whether you help us or not. Although it is foretold that you do, that can change if you decide you cannot. I hope to see you again tomorrow."

Peter slithered down to the ground and gave McDragon's scaley leg a pat, then glancing over his shoulder he hurried as fast as he could back to the house, feeling very hungry. He had been away a long time despite it being in dragon time.

CHAPTER SEVEN

The beach held lots of fascinating finds for Alice and Peter who spent most of the day scrabbling around looking for booty which was washed up on the beach. Peter was very pleased to find that he was not tired by all his dragon travels and he still had lots of energy. It seemed it was just his hunger that was affected.

He found a bright red buoy which he guessed used to hold a lobster pot in place. Callum had pointed out the buoys bobbing about on the surface of the sea as they had passed them. What's more Peter now knew that the fishermen used salt herring as the bait for the feisty but tasty lobsters. The unsuspecting lobsters scrambled into the tunnels inside the pots to eat the feast left in there for them and couldn't get out again.

Some of the buoys had numbers on them so the fisherman knew which boat they belonged to.

As the pair of them were foraging a loud splosh in the sea made them both turn to look. Suddenly a very large white bird popped up onto the surface gobbling down a fish. Then it took off to fly high in the air. It looked rather like a glider and as they watched it went into a very steep fast dive to enter the water very elegantly making the sea splash up around it. It was a very big bird indeed.

Peter wracked his brains, he knew he had heard something about these birds and then he announced proudly, "Gannets, that's what they are. Gannets!"

Alice was unimpressed, she was more interested in watching the crab she could see crawling about in the bottom of a rock pool.

Peter spotted something blue caught around a rock and when he went to investigate he found a good length rope which must have come off a yacht for some reason or other. It had quite a good sized pulley attached to it. He added it to their pile of finds.

It was hungry work looking for goodies on the beach and they eventually made their way back to the house for a snack. When they opened the door a series of delicious smells wafted towards them. Mum had been baking.

"Those look nice mum, can we try some?" Peter asked indicating a pile of scones.

"Yes, have some jam with them. They are just out of the oven."

They washed the scones down with milk. Just what the doctor ordered to keep empty tummies going until lunch time.

Peter gave a contented sigh.

"You look happy young man."

"I like it here mum, I'm glad we came."

"That's because Biffy isn't here!" Alice mumbled knowingly through a mouthful.

"Don't speak with your mouth full Alice!" Then, "Who

is Biffy? I don't remember you mentioning him before Peter. Is he a friend of yours?"

"Not really."

"You never talk about your friends at school, perhaps you could ask Biffy to tea one day."

Peter's face was a picture, he couldn't think of anything he'd like less, but he really didn't want to talk to his mum about it as that would mean telling her about the bullying. Luckily the buzzer on the cooker went off and mum was soon engrossed in removing more cakes from the oven which gave Peter a chance to nip outside in case she questioned him some more.

As Alice seemed happy to stay inside and help, Peter thought he'd pay a visit to McDragon but although he scrambled over the rocks calling, the dragon did not wake. Peter sat down and rested his back against the big body and watched the gannets diving into the bay. Then he started to talk, even though it was unlikely that McDragon was listening. Alice's mention of Biffy's name had brought the tension he usually felt at school back into his whole body and he had the need to offload to someone, even if McDragon was asleep.

He told his dragon friend all about Biffy and his cronies and how they picked on him every day while he was at school, waiting for him to arrive and ambushing him on his way home. He tried to dodge them but they always seemed to know where he was going to be.

"School would be alright without them," he said quietly. "I cannot tell mum or dad because that might make the problem even bigger than it is. I just pretend I'm very clumsy and keep falling over and bruising myself.

I often don't get to eat my lunch because Biffy manages to knock it out of my hand or do something to it. It's no wonder I'm small for my age. I wish I knew what it is about me that he doesn't like."

He jumped with fright as a big voice boomed through his head.

"Perhaps you have something this Biffy is jealous of?"

"Oh!! I didn't think you could hear me!"

"Oh yes, Petersmith, I can hear you very well even if I am not in my dragon form."

"Well, Biffy calls me the Crip or Cripple because of my hand so he couldn't be jealous of me."

"Maybe you have something in your life that he doesn't have. Perhaps you should feel sorry for him, not for yourself. He can't be very happy with life if he has to be horrid all the time. You seem to me to be a very able and happy fellow with a loving family."

"I am NOT sorry for myself! I'll maybe see you tomorrow!" shouted Peter as he scrambled angrily down the rocks, grazing his legs on the rough stones. Why should he feel sorry for Biffy, Peter was the one who was being bullied.

He couldn't go across the beach to the cottage because while he had been talking the sea had crept in, so he went the long way round past the end of McDragon's long tail and up over the tiny bridge which crossed the burn. He stopped on the bridge to reach down into the clear water and scooped some up with his hand to splash it into his mouth. It dribbled down his chin but it tasted delicious and fresh. Then he scooted along the grassy path to the house.

He cheered up when he saw his dad walking from the direction of the car across the cliff and he made a detour to meet him so they could walk to the house together. He wished he could tell his dad about McDragon and also about Biffy, but he knew that he could not do that, and anyway his dad might think he was making both stories up.

CHAPTER EIGHT

Peter stretched out in his bed – it was early again but this morning was different because he was going out on one of the big speed boats with his dad. His dad was going to interview a chap called Murdo McMuran and do some research of some archives he had there. They were going to a tiny island in the middle of nowhere. He hadn't had time to let McDragon know because his dad had only asked him if he wanted to go with him just before bed.

There was a light tap on the door and dad poked his head around it and said quietly, "We need to leave soon Peter, can you get ready quickly?"

"Sure dad," and in a flash he was up, washed, dressed and fed and before he knew it they were on the way in the car to where they had to pick up the boat.

His dad was quite right, the boat journey took a couple of hours and Peter spent most of the time on the bow deck facing forward with the salty spray spattering onto his face. It was exciting and he kept licking his lips as he quite liked the taste of the seawater. Luckily, he had his hood pulled up so apart from his face he didn't get wet. He imagined he was a pirate on his way to find some treasure and kept muttering, "Fee fi fo fum and a bottle of rum!" and "Walk the plank me hearties!"

The boat took them past some big rocky stacks standing up incredibly high out of the sea where the gannets were diving down in their hundreds and coming up with fish in their beaks. Pirates forgotten, Peter snapped away happily with his camera as the captain slowed down to show them the thousands and thousands of sea birds which lived on these very tall statuesque rocks. Then they were off again – full speed ahead.

Eventually the roar of the engine slowed down again and the spray from the bow lessened and gradually died off. Peter was astounded to see absolutely huge rocky cliffs towering vertically out of the sea causing an enormous shadow on the waves. The island in front of them made the previous rock stacks look miniscule. As they sailed into the shadow they changed direction and suddenly the vista in front of them changed. Peter's mouth went into a big "O". The island stretched a long way ahead – they must have approached from the narrow end of the island but in reality it was like a huge oval with towering cliffs surrounding it. The boat headed towards a shadowy gap in the rocks and a sailor came close to him and picked up one of the ropes which was looped in a tidy pile at the prow of the deck near to where Peter was standing. He smiled at Peter and laughingly said as he pointed high above them, "I hope you have lots of energy young man! See the top of these cliffs? Well that's where you have to climb as Murdo McMuran's house is right at the very top!"

"Gosh! How do we get up there?"

Peter's dad answered as he came out of the boat's cabin to join him, "We walk son, we walk."

They stood together watching the sailor work. Inside the inlet the sun shone down from above making it quite warm and sheltered while the boat chugged along slowly until finally it came to a smooth halt to allow the sailor to leap over to the small jetty and tie the boat up neatly alongside using the big rusty metal rings that were welded into the stone. Peter and his dad waited for their instructions to disembark, chatting together quietly.

"I'm sure that Murdo won't mind you exploring while we're here Peter, otherwise you might get a bit bored. Just remember not to go to the edge of any cliffs please, your mum would kill me if anything happened to you!"

"I won't do anything silly dad, don't worry. I'm sure there is lots to see to keep me occupied and I've got my camera with me." Then he giggled, "Lucky Alice wasn't with us for that boat ride!"

His dad grinned back at him, "Well she definitely won't be a sailor when she grows up, that's for sure!"

Peter's legs felt a bit wobbly when he finally stepped onto dry land but fortunately one of the seamen gave him a helping hand. He didn't feel so silly when he saw that his dad also had to have a little help.

At the bottom of the steep stone steps they both stopped and stared upwards. The steps seemed to go on forever. There was an old rope handrail to the left hand side to hang on to if they needed it. They thanked the captain and the sailors and both looked hesitantly upwards, each adjusting their backpacks. There was enough light coming down from the very top for them to see the worn stone stairs which were beginning to spiral their way upwards.

"I'm going to feel a bit like Jack and the Beanstalk climbing up that high!" said his dad and Peter giggled nervously in response.

"So long as there's not a giant at the top!"

Taking in a deep breath they started their long journey upwards. Half way up they stopped to mop their brows.

"A lift would be good here!" muttered Peter.

"Too right. Well at least we're getting some exercise, some people would pay a lot of money for that!"

When they finally reached the top of the steps they were both puffing very hard – it had been an incredibly long climb. While they had a brief rest to try and regain their breath Peter looked around. There was a large single storey old stone house not far from where they were standing and they soon set off again, both rather red in the face. As they neared it the huge wooden door at the front of the building creaked open and a man dressed in a purple coloured kilt with a green jacket stepped out to greet them and shook Peter's dad's hand enthusiastically. His dad introduced him to Peter and Peter immediately offered his hand ready to politely shake the man's hand. As they touched he felt a strange prickly tingling at the back of his neck and it took a big effort not to drop the man's hand immediately. For some reason his instinct told him not to let the shock that he felt show on his face so he forced himself to smile limply and released his grip as soon as he could. Very strange!

They were waved into the house and offered refreshments but Peter felt very reluctant to go over the threshold and asked if he could explore outside instead. "I have my sandwiches with me and a drink in my back pack and I promise not to go near the edge of any cliffs. I bet there must be a lot of interesting birds to see up this high."

His father looked enquiringly at Mr McMuran who nodded his head slowly in agreement.

"The only thing I would say laddie, is that it is best to keep out of the wooded part of the island should you come across it. There are quite a few dead trees in there and I wouldn't like you to get hit on the head by a falling branch."

"No problem sir, if I do find it I'll keep away from it." He turned to look at his dad, "What time shall I come back here dad?"

"As the boat is coming for us at three thirty I think you should be back half an hour earlier than that, just to be on the safe side. A word of warning though when you are near the cliffs keep an eye out for the big skuas. They will dive bomb you if you go too close to their nests and they can be quite scary sea birds."

"Ok dad, I'll be careful," and with a quick smile Peter scampered away feeling a great relief to be away from Mr McMuran. That tingling feeling at the back of his neck was a bit worrying.

The next hour was spent happily exploring the long tall island. He had not seen any sign of the woods that the kilted man had told him might not be safe and he was quite content keeping to the cliff edges as he searched for birds whilst laying on his tummy and peering down through his small binoculars where he could see many of the sea birds sitting on their nests, squawking loudly when another bird got near them or else they were flying out to sea and diving down into the murky depths to pop up again with a fish in their beaks. Every so often he would check in the little bird book he had brought with him to see what species he was observing.

The island was big enough for him to have covered only part of it when he sat on a log looking out to sea munching away on some of his sandwiches. His watch told him it was only noon and quite early to eat but he was feeling a bit peckish as they had been up very early that morning and there'd only been time for some cereals before they set off along the cliff top to the car.

His head was constantly on the move, looking this way and that fascinated by the bird life around him.

"Oh, what's that over there?" he muttered to himself snatching up his binoculars. "Oh, it's only a crow!" As he twisted back towards his pack he overbalanced and tumbled down a long grassy slope dropping his binoculars on the way.

He finally came to rest against something rather jelly like that stretched from the ground upwards. He tested it with his hand.

"That's very strange!" he struggled to right himself looking upwards as he did, "and where on earth did that slope come from. I never saw it before I fell." As he rather shakily stood up trying to fathom whether he was hurt anywhere he wobbled a bit and his arm went out to balance himself, his hand pressing slightly on the jelly like almost cobwebby substance which had stopped his fall. With a pop his hand and arm disappeared.

"Ohh!! Where's my hand?!" He flexed his fingers, he

could still feel them but just not see them so he pulled his arm back towards him and with another little pop, he was whole again.

"How weird is that?" He leaned forward and pushed gently against the membrane like substance which was repelling him, watching his arm disappearing, at the same time he stepped forward to balance himself a little more and there was a slightly louder pop! He was through it – but where on earth was he? It was dark and gloomy and there were tall trees everywhere. Where had the sun gone? He looked back to where he had come through. There was nothing to see at all!

CHAPTER NINE

"I wonder if these are the woods that I'm supposed to keep out of?" His neck still tingled.

The semi-darkness was really very scary and just as he was considering trying to return to the sunshine he got the feeling that someone or something was watching him. He spun his gaze this way and that but he couldn't see anyone near him and the air smelt of damp pine needles and something else… something almost animally. There was no bird song. It was incredibly eerie and he felt very uncomfortable and a little frightened. It seemed he was in a kind of dome because the trees at the edge where he had entered were much shorter than the ones he could see further into the gloom.

It really did feel like something was looking at him? He couldn't see anyone or anything. His neck prickled some more and he shivered.

Straight in front of him were two enormous fallen tree trunks about three metres long and about a metre in diameter. They each had a couple of branches pointing out bending slightly upwards from one end, rather like horns.

At the other end roots dangled downwards almost as if they were tails. Both trunks had a woody knot in roughly the same place not far from the look-a-like horns which gave them the appearance of having an eye, and it was as if they were facing each other. Maybe the logs were thinking of having a wrestling match. Peter grinned at the thought.

As he studied them he jumped, he felt sure one of them had blinked at him!

"Silly me, don't be such a scaredy cat! You're imagining things! I'd best get out of here and back to my lunch and the sunshine."

As he thought that, both of the fallen trunks turned to stare straight at him. Ooer, the knots he could see were eyes and they had them both sides of their heads! He stepped backwards and fell over into a pile of dirty pine needles. One of the trunk like beings stepped forward and then took another step and the second trunk thing followed it! Peter jumped to his feet and ran. He could hear them lumbering heavily behind him. It sounded like a herd of elephants on his tail. He stopped to draw in a big breath and then pounded forwards into the depths of the forest and away from the safety of the sunshine outside.

Finally, Peter had to come to a halt, he was panting heavily and he knew he couldn't go any further until he had caught his breath again. He felt as bad as he had after climbing all of those stone steps from the jetty. He nervously checked behind him wiping his brow with his hand. He had sweat dripping down his face but there was no sign of anything following him so maybe he'd out run them. Thank goodness for that!

As he bent over to try and relieve the stitch that he had

in his side he heard a buzzing sound coming from over to the left.

"Oh please! I can't run anymore!" he muttered to himself peering around to where the sound was coming from. It seemed to be a mound of what looked like composting leaves and pine needles and suddenly they lifted off the ground, rather like a hovercraft would. The mound was about a metre in diameter. Could he possibly run again? He stood up straight to get ready to try to set off again but then gave out a big breath of relief when the mound subsided back down to the ground. Once it was settled he could see there were thousands and thousands of huge winged ant-like insects amongst the pine needles and dust. It was definitely time to try and get out of here!

The tree canopy above him was very dense and he felt quite scared when he realised that he'd lost his way completely. He had absolutely no idea how to get back to where he had entered this horrible place. He thought he'd come from behind, but in his panic he hadn't paid any attention to his direction. He knew with certainty that he didn't want to venture anywhere near the trunk like creatures again and what's more he was definitely not going to get too close to the ant pile either.

He could feel his breathing getting faster and faster as he started to panic and then shake with fear. No-one would know where he was, what was he going to do?!

"I am the one chosen by the dragons to help save them and they wouldn't be in a panic!" he told himself in a loud voice and then tried to slow his breathing down like he had seen his mum do when she was getting cross about something. "Right, I will walk slowly and carefully away from this mound of ants!"

"Dragons?" asked a voice which boomed into his head and Peter jumped in fright again.

"Wh..oo..oo are you?! Where are you?"

"I'm behind you! Do be careful of the antors, if they decide to attack you they can be very nasty and they can immerse you and gobble you up in no time at all! Trust me, I know, I've seen it happen! There would be nothing left of you – not a scrap."

Keeping half an eye on the antors Peter turned around very slowly – right up close to him he could see two large nostrils and two big amethyst eyes peering at him from a scaly head the size of a pony's. As Peter examined this creature he saw a long neck with spines standing up along its crest, and there were interlocking dark grey scales with a green tinge at their edges running down the whole length of the neck and body ending in a big tail.

"Wow! Another dragon!" he muttered.

"Another dragon! Do you mean there are others like me?" and a cloud of dust and pine needles were scattered into the air as the small dragon's tail swept along the ground in excitement. The dragon started to make little bounces on his short stubby legs, his talons sinking into the dead pine needles beneath him as he did. Peter began to cough and splutter and had to hold his hands over his mouth so he could breathe.

"Can you stop that please, I can't breathe!"

"Oops, sorry!"

Gradually as the dragon stopped his little jumps the

51

dust and pine needles settled back down and Peter could take his hands away from his mouth.

"You said another dragon!"

"Yes, you're the third dragon I've met, although the others were very, very large so I guess they are a lot older than you. The first one is called McDragon and the other one is Haribald d'Ness. He lives in Loch Ness!" Peter announced importantly. "What's more there is another dragon I've not met yet called Seraphina. I'm supposed to be helping them find Seraphina's lost Pearl so that the dragons do not die out! Not that I know how to…" he finished quietly.

The little dragon started to bounce about on his stubby legs again and swish his tail began about.

"Please don't do that," Peter asked as he began to cough again.

"Oh sorry. Three more dragons! I would love to see them!"

The dust was beginning to subside once more.

"I'm sure they would be happy to meet you as well, but first of all I would need to get out of here and I'm a little lost. I don't want to meet up with those enormous tree beings again!"

"You mean the mamothias. They don't eat meat so you're safe but they do have a very nasty bite if they decide to attack you." The dragon's voice spoke in Peter's head, just the same as McDragon's did when he was with him.

"But how would I explain it if they bit me – I'm not supposed to be in here and I'll get in trouble. Can you help me please?"

All of a sudden Peter was knocked down to the ground.

"Ahh! What did…" a scaly tail pushed against his mouth and the dragon muttered softly, "Be quiet! Don't move at all!"

Peter froze where he was and tried to see what the dragon was hiding him from. He caught a glimpse of something or somebody walking in a slithery way not too far in front of the dragon. The dragon had a strange look on his face that made Peter want to giggle. It seemed the dragon was trying to look like a picture of innocence. Then Peter heard the person moving away from them.

"Phew!" muttered the dragon, "You wouldn't want to meet him at any time!"

"Who or what was he?"

"He's called Slider, and he reports back to the boss. He knows everything that goes on in here and he's a nasty piece of work. I don't like him. He's a bully, and he likes to torment me and call me names when he brings me my food."

Peter scrabbled back onto his feet dusting himself off as he did so. His head was full of questions but he really felt manners might be in order here.

"How do you do? I'm Peter Smith, and I am pleased to meet you. What's your name?"

The dragon looked a little shamefaced and then said, "Slider calls me Wee Spittle, but I hate that name!"

"Well what is your name?"

"Spit!!" the dragon announced bouncing on all four feet as he did but fortunately this time it was not accompanied by a swishing tail.

"I shall call you Spit McDragon as you are a Scottish dragon!"

"I like that very much," was the proud response.

"But why does he call you Wee Spittle?"

Spit looked down at the ground and then said, "This is why," and he puffed himself up and then blew hard through his nostrils. As he did a shower of sparks spurted out followed by a lot of green snot which promptly put the sparks out. "I am sure I am supposed to be able to breathe fire, but all I seem to puff out is gunge and a few sparks." Peter felt a giggle start to bubble up inside him and move up into his mouth and he bit down hard to stop it. He realised that if he did laugh he would cause offence. He masked it with a cough instead.

"I bet if you keep practising you'll finally manage to. Don't be sad about the nickname, I have a nickname too. At school they call me the Crip – which is short for cripple and this is why." He showed his left hand to Spit and then he held his other hand out as well so the dragon could see the difference, "See, I only have two fingers and a thumb on this hand," he said waving it about in the air.

"Will they grow back?"

"No, never. I was born like it, but I can manage alright, it's just a little trickier picking some things up with that hand and buttoning shirts up. I hate being called the Crip, so we both have nicknames we don't like."

Spit touched Peter on the head with his nose very gently as if to be sympathetic.

"The dragons call me Petersmith!" he announced proudly.

"Well, Petersmith, it's nice to have a friend, I have never had one before," the dragon said softly.

"I have a couple of so called friends at school but

they're scared of Biffy, he's the one who named me the Crip, so they won't hang about with me if he or his cronies are about. I don't know why he picks on me but Biffy always manages to knock my food onto the floor at lunch time and I rarely get to eat it."

"I wouldn't like someone to mess with my food!" at that thought Spit looked very much like a very fierce dragon. "Would you like to go exploring with me Petersmith?"

"Well, that might be fun but I do need to find the way out of here. I came here with my dad and I have to get back in time to catch the boat." He glanced at the watch on his wrist, "But I have a little time to stay with you."

"I can help you leave when the time comes. I will be able to follow the trail you left when the mamothias chased you."

Peter felt a rush of air go past his head and he ducked.

"Whoops, I need to introduce you to Archie, he is my friend!"

"Who is Archie?"

A large black crow landed on Spit's head and opened his big black beak and cawed very loudly. Unusually he had a streak of white down one wing.

"Hi, Archie, I believe I saw you outside in the sunshine." Archie cawed in response.

"Archie gets bullied too. The other crows don't like the white on his body so they bomb him when he is flying near them. He gets covered in cuts and bruises if he doesn't get away in time so he spends a lot of his time in here with me."

"That's terrible! So, bullying seems to happen to birds, dragons and boys then. Where shall we go? I must be careful because I was told to keep out of here."

Spit started to bounce about – it seemed that he got very excited very easily.

"Let's go this way!" he said, "just keep beside me and talk quietly as we don't want anyone else to see you and while we walk you can tell me all about the dragons you have met. Archie will fly in front of us as a spy." Archie cawed again and pushed off the dragon's head to fly off ahead of them.

CHAPTER TEN

Peter woke the next morning feeling quite happy and contented. He thought excitedly of his new friends, Spit and Archie. They had done lots of exploring. Peter would hide whenever Archie flew back uttering his big warning cry, which was two loud squawks, to let them know there were predators about. Once they had spotted Slider in the distance but he was too far away to see them. It had been great fun. They'd had a few mock fights, scuffling about in the pine needles together. Spit seemed to really enjoy it and Peter couldn't remember another time when he had done that with anyone other than his dad. You always knew when Spit was about to pounce though, because he uttered a kind of dragon giggle before he moved.

From what Spit said there was a lot more of the bubble dome to explore as it was far bigger than it appeared. Peter guessed that was due to some sort of magic. Strange how he took magic for granted now he'd met McDragon.

His new pals had eventually taken him back to the spot where he had entered through the jelly like substance. Spit used his big nose to follow the tracks Peter had left when he had been running. The mamothias were nowhere to be seen. Sadly, it seemed that Spit couldn't leave the area, the jelly barrier stopped him, but it didn't trouble Archie who could escape in the same way that Peter did. They made a plan that Spit would come to the same spot each day at roughly the same time in the hope that Peter could come back to play again.

He had felt the same little tug and pop when he pushed through out into the sunshine to clamber back up the long slope. It hadn't taken him long at all to pick up his bag and scrabble around until he found his fallen binoculars and then run back to meet his dad, Archie flying high above him.

Archie settled himself in a nearby tree to watch Peter running over to his dad and it had been a great relief to find that Mr McMuran was nowhere in sight. The trek down the steep steps seemed a lot quicker than the journey up.

Back on the boat his dad said he would not be returning the next day as he had some other work to do, but he was very pleased that Peter had enjoyed himself enough to ask to tag along next time.

* * *

The following morning Peter couldn't wait to tell McDragon all about his new mate and it wasn't long before he was rushing across the little beach and clambering up the rocks, his temper tantrum of the other day forgotten.

He smiled when he saw the dragon was waiting for him, this time in dragon form, and before he could get across the rocks McDragon had launched himself into the air and circled above Peter's head. His wings buffeted the air and Peter had to brace himself in case he was blown over. Eventually McDragon landed quite lightly next to him on the beach which was amazing considering he was such a big beast. He was so very much larger than Spit.

"How are you today Petersmith?"

"I am very well, thank you," he answered politely and then rushed excitedly into all that had happened to him yesterday. As he finished his tale McDragon had a very thoughtful expression on his big face.

"What do you think McDragon? Where did Spit come from, because he doesn't know?"

"I am not at all sure Petersmith; it's a mystery to me!"

"Do you think the drawings in the cave might show us something? It was such a quick visit last time so we didn't study the pictures for long and you said they often change. They may give us some ideas for my quest, although I'm not at all sure if I am capable of taking it on."

"That's a good idea Petersmith, hop on board and let's be off."

Before Peter knew it they were flying above the clouds racing up higher and higher making the lochs below them look like tiny puddles surrounded by green and brown. The cold air was rushing through Peter's hair but he was as warm as toast because McDragon had breathed heat on him before they had left and it lingered nicely in his body.

Suddenly McDragon's whole body jarred and if the scales hadn't been over his knees holding Peter into place he would have come right off the dragon's back.

They started to spiral downwards, the air rushing against his body and head and making it feel as if it were pulling Peter's hair out from its roots. They were spinning and spinning and Peter felt his stomach almost come up into his mouth. He was screaming as they hurtled towards the ground. McDragon was fighting hard to gain control as he powered his huge wings up and down trying desperately to straighten them up.

Out of the corner of his eye Peter saw something large and very red come at them at a tremendous pace.

"What is it?" he yelled.

"You mean they! They are two squawkins, evil creatures who were spawned at the same time as the dragons. They crave dragon blood. Mind their talons, remember I told you the poison in them could kill you." After a few nail biting seconds McDragon seemed to gain control and they flattened out to move them forward rather than downwards.

"I'll have to fly hard and fast to get away from them." And they surged onward.

Peter wasn't sure if he was more excited or scared as McDragon dodged this way and that.

"Look out to the rear!" he shouted and moments later the dragon's tail sideswiped the red beast pursuing them. It must have taken it by surprise because the squawkin started to spin towards the ground twisting round and round as it did, terrifying screams coming from it, so bad that Peter had to put his fingers in his ears.

"That is why they are called squawkins, Petersmith! It is a terrible sound indeed."

"The other one seems to be following the first one down and something very big has appeared and is chasing after them!"

"Hmm, something big you say, I wonder what that is? Thank you, your warning came just in time. Now we might be able to continue unhindered."

"But won't they be waiting for us when we return?"

"I think it is unlikely laddie because it will take the one I whacked a while to recover.

"Are they really flying gargoyles?"

"Yes, you could put it that way." Peter could feel the smile on McDragon's face as he answered.

"Dragons on the other hand will always remain as they are now. They will not change in any way at all. That is our strength."

There was silence for a while apart from the wind whistling in Peter's ears. Surprisingly he still felt nice and warm again and his breathing had settled down because he felt quite safe.

Peter turned to look behind them and out of nowhere the "something large" which he had seen before was racing up towards McDragon's tail. It was going so fast he couldn't see what it was.

"Behind you again!" he shouted, but this time McDragon did not change direction or pace, he just turned and said, "Well met Seraphina! I am glad to see you!"

Seraphina hummed in reply.

Peter was stunned… so this was Seraphina and it was she who had been chasing after the squawkins.

"Petersmith! I am so pleased to meet you at last!"

"And I y…you." he stuttered as he stared at the pale dragon who had a turquoise sheen to her, like the colour of a Carribean sea and who was now flying in tandem with them. She was slightly smaller than McDragon.

McDragon was humming… he seemed happy and his body thrummed with the sound. Seraphina could be heard humming as well.

"I have been aware of your arrival for some while Petersmith and I knew the time would soon be upon us when I would get to meet you. You have given me hope at long last."

"Oh wow!" Peter found the strength to answer. "But I don't know why I should be the person chosen to do this q… quest." he stuttered. "I am only a small boy with a crippled hand – I am not really fit for this task."

"Petersmith, you must believe in yourself. You are the chosen one."

"But w…why?"

"The seer who makes the predictions has said so. Maybe it is because you believe in dragons and most humans do not."

"Well, I have always believed in dragons and I am honoured to meet you all," he announced bending his head. "But how will I find the Pearl when I am not allowed to go out without my parents!" His voice was getting stronger as he was feeling more resentful of this task.

"McDragon will help you and you will search in dragon time. Without your help dragons may cease to exist as I am one of the last few female dragons left in Scotland. I have sworn never to lay another Pearl until my first one is found, so we need your help as I cannot break my oath. I made it in a moment of deep distress and now it is too late to reverse it. It is written in the dragon seer's caves that Petersmith will help save our kind."

Seraphina had an almost smug look on her large

dragon face as the three of them proceeded higher and higher up to the dragon cave. "I can see you are heading towards the seer's cave. I shall come with you as who knows what we may see. It's so good to be up in the sky again after being in a state rather like hibernation."

CHAPTER ELEVEN

Peter tried not to worry when he noticed they were nearly at the cave mouth again, remembering all too well their first landing in the entrance. He braced himself for a choppy landing and put his head down on the scaly neck as he felt his big friend's wings move very slowly and gracefully before he folded them tightly against his body and went into an angled dive directly into the dark fissure in the wall of grey rock. As soon as McDragon entered the cave, he lowered his legs and his talons rasped on the rocky floor as he pounded down the passageway gradually slowing into a measured walk.

"Wow, that was a good entrance!" said Peter admiringly. "One of your best landings so far."

"Hurumph!" was all the answer he got.

Peter slipped down and they walked side by side along the tunnel. He heard Seraphina arrive behind them, her talons scratching on the ground.

When they finally reached the murals this time it was Seraphina who talked Peter through them. Even though he had seen them before he studied them closely and noticed just how much detail they had in them.

"You can see from the magicians' faces the pure anger they were feeling against one another and how fierce the fighting was. Then, in this next etching you see the gargoyles being released from their stones and coming to life? As McDragon has told you they have become squawkins and they are not something you would want to meet without a dragon by your side."

Seraphina turned to look at him as they continued down the passageway past other murals showing more of the war between the magicians. Peter almost felt she was trying to gauge his thoughts.

They stopped by a picture of Seraphina herself and Haribald d'Ness who were both looking between some rocks on the ground. They had rather soft soppy expressions on their faces.

Seraphina gave a big dragon sigh next to him "Ah Haribald…, I have so missed him!" And then a deep sadness came into her voice, "And there is my beautiful Pearl!" and Peter looked up at her and was shocked to see big dragon tears running down her face and splashing down to make puddles on the rocky ground. He looked back at the mural where on the ground between the rocks he could just see a grey pebble flecked with blue about the size of an ostrich egg. At least he had finally seen a dragon's Pearl so that was something positive from this trip. He wondered again how on earth he would find it.

"There, there Seraphina." rumbled McDragon, "It will be alright. Just you wait and see."

Further along they came to another etching containing Peter and Spit standing next to one another. It most definitely had not been there before or Peter was sure he would have noticed it. Archie was perched on Spit's head looking much like a black hat and Peter giggled when he saw it.

"And that, Petersmith, must be your new-found friend, but unfortunately the pictures do not give us a clue as to where he comes from. He cannot have been Seraphina's Pearl because Seraphina knows her Pearl contains a female dragon. To find out more we would need to bring Spit, as you call him, here to the dragon seer's cave where each dragon has a different story board to see. His tale will only appear to him, but for all that he must be part of your quest because he is drawn here with you."

All Peter could do was look amazed at the thought of this.

"Spit would love to know more, I'm sure!"

There was silence for a while apart from a "Hmm," from Seraphina and Peter guessed that McDragon was communicating with her, possibly explaining Peter's story of his exploits from yesterday.

Seraphina blew out a deep breath and wet splattered the rocks by the side of them as she did. "But who is that, he looks very familiar?" and her long snout touched the back of another drawing which Peter did not remember from his previous visit.

He drew closer and saw two men standing there. He was shocked to see that one was his father and the other, wearing a purple kilt, was Mr McMuran.

"My dad is the one on the left and the other one is Mr McMuran. He owns the island and invited my dad to go there – something to do with dad's work, although I don't know what that is."

Both dragons stared for a while at the drawing.

"Hmmmm, yes there is something about him... not your dad, Petersmith, but the other man."

Peter shrugged and moved on past the dragons where he stopped in shock, "Look! Look at this!"

In front of him he could see Mr McMuran looking furious and suddenly there was a big flash from Mr McMuran's finger which was pointing out of the picture straight at Peter. The dragons leapt backwards totally surprised by the flame that shot towards them as the smell of singed hair filled the air.

"Ow!" Peter's voice squeaked with fear.

"I've never ever seen a picture move like that. Look, the flame has scorched a bit of your hair!" McDragon seemed totally dumbfounded, as did Seraphina. "That is definitely a grave warning!"

"I wondered why I'd felt a tingle when I shook his hand – he must be a wrong un! What is in the next picture?"

They all looked and there was Petersmith weaving through tall trees with Spit a few metres away. Peter was looking over his shoulder at something behind them. He had fear on his face but they could not see what it was they were running from.

"This is another drawing which was not there when we last looked. Definitely, you must be careful Petersmith!"

Peter was silent all the way back to the house. Seraphina flew with them and landed on the rocks in the small bay. Peter had been deep in thought on the journey and finally he came to a decision. Once he was on his own two feet he drew himself up as tall as he could and stared up at both of the dragons.

"I must carry out my quest! It would be a terrible happening if in time dragons ceased to exist!" he announced. "Also, I must help my new friend Spit escape what is like a prison to him!"

The two dragons nodded in unison and Seraphina answered, "Thank you Petersmith, right from the bottom of my dragon heart! I am sure that your friend Spit has something to do with my lost Pearl but you must always be on your guard." As she spoke she bent her neck so that her nose touched her chest.

"Touch me here!" she commanded. Peter put his hand on her big scaly front as she told him to wrap his fingers around a scale and pull hard. The scale came away in his hand. She prodded his forehead with her snout and he felt a prickle at the base of his neck as she did. When she took her head away he could feel the spot on his forehead tingling and warm. The scale felt very pliable and soft in his hand.

"This is my gift for you Petersmith. Keep it safe and with you always. Now I have dragon burnt you I will be able to sense you, Petersmith, through the scale. If you are in danger or need me, hold it and think of me, and I will come as fast as the wind to aid you. You are now dragon kin and this is our secret!"

"Wow!!! And wow!!! Thank you, Seraphina! I promise I will not tell a soul about this."

"Thank you Petersmith, you are an amazing and brave boy! Remember that the seer's pictures show that you find my Pearl and I believe you will!"

McDragon smiled benignly at him and started to hum and Seraphina joined in the humming. It was a very comforting sound and Peter felt himself relax at what must be some kind of dragon song. He bowed low to show his appreciation.

"I must go now!" he said, "I will visit the island with my dad next time he is due there and I will make sure I take your gift with me in case I need you Seraphina."

CHAPTER TWELVE

When Peter burst through the front door, thanks to dragon time, it looked like his mum had only just started cooking their breakfast. He was starving and grabbed a piece of bread and butter which was on a plate on the table.

"Where have you been Peter?" she asked.

"Oh, just down to the rocks, I like exploring there and looking out for the otter and at the seabirds. I really like it here mum but the sea air makes me very, very hungry!"

The bacon started to spit in the pan and it smelled wonderful and he felt he was an incredibly happy bunny when he was able to tuck into his eggs and bacon. His plate was nearly as full as his dad's.

"Your dad has time to take us all out this morning. We thought we would go to Luskentyre which is a smashing sandy beach."

"That sounds good mum."

"After that we'll drive to Leverburgh and see one of the scallop fishermen there. It would be good if we could have some scallops for supper tonight. They are a real treat to eat. You'll like them, they taste very sweet." said his father as he ruffled his son's mop of hair, "Mum is making a bigger lunch than normal because you seem to eat so much more up here. It must be all that fresh air. I've never known you to be outside for such a long time each day."

"Mmmm," agreed Peter hastily shovelling another piece of toast into his mouth so he wouldn't look guilty. His dad had no idea of his other dragon life. He needed sustenance to keep his energy levels up.

He watched his mum padding about the kitchen making a variety of baps filled with corned beef, egg and ham with salad. Then much to his approval she packed a whole fruit cake which she had baked the day before, and finally added some fruit.

"Mum?"

"Yes, Peter?"

"Do you think dragons could really have existed?"

Mum didn't even hesitate, "It would be strange if they didn't, simply because how else would all the books about dragons have come about. What's more I think it is dragon country up here!" She smiled at him.

Peter glanced across at his dad who was watching them and rolling his eyes in disbelief, but Peter was happy with his mum's answer. It was good to know that if push came to shove she might believe him, not that he could tell her of course, because he had made the promise to McDragon and Seraphina not to tell a soul.

Alice rushed into the room clutching her camera. "Are we nearly ready to go?"

"Eat something first please madam!" ordered mum and Peter took the opportunity to bound up the stairs to his room to gather his camera and the small pair of

71

binoculars which his grandfather had given to him. He hung the binoculars around his neck and pushed the camera deep into his pocket. His bird book was also an essential item to take.

Once Alice had eaten some toast they started the walk to the car with dad carrying the rucksack containing the lunch. Peter looked across through his binoculars to McDragon's rocks and he could have sworn the sleeping dragon winked at him.

Alice found it a boring trip and spent much of her time asking when they were going to get there. At least she wasn't sick. He, on the other hand was fascinated by the landscape and was trying to imprint it on his memory so he might know it if they flew over it at any time. As the car wended its way towards Luskentyre his dad pulled over and pointed out a pair of golden eagles circling above them. Peter snatched up his binoculars to stare at them wondering if he and McDragon had flown above them at all. He had no idea at all – and certainly no idea about where the seer's cave was.

The tide was on its way out when they arrived and a beautiful beach was in front of them, looking much like one that could be in Greece or somewhere exotic. He and Alice ran full pelt along the lovely sands, splashing about in the sea water as they ran through the edge of the sea.

Mum and dad had said they would meet them over to the right hand side of the beach amongst the rocks and when the children arrived there they were delighted to see a large assortment of beautiful large pebbles which the lowering tide was revealing. Peter looked at them and thought, "Surely the Pearl is not hidden here! How can I ever sort through this many rocks!" He touched on the soft scale in his pocket and nearly overbalanced on the rock he was standing on as a gentle dragon voice came to him.

"Petersmith, do not worry about the stones you can see, they are just rocks and the Pearl is not there. Enjoy your time with the stones, you never know some of them might have magic in them!" and he heard a soft chuckle.

He felt the panic leave him. "Was that you Seraphina?" he thought.

"Yes. We will meet again soon Petersmith. I forgot to tell you that we could speak to each other through the scale when you touch it." And he felt her voice fading away and he was alone with his thoughts again.

"Are you OK Peter?" asked his dad who had noticed the shocked expression on Peter's face.

"Yes, thanks dad. I was just amazed to see such beautiful rocks." That was true at least, he thought to himself.

"Well, lad, there used to be far more of them than this but visitors have been taking them as souvenirs. Maybe at some point there will be a sign asking people to leave them here before they all disappear."

Peter and Alice scrambled inelegantly across the rocks, making sure their feet didn't slip into any of the crevices between them. At the far edge they found that people had balanced stones on top of each other to make a sort of totem pole and the children decided to each leave a tower of pebbles of their own. It was not as easy as it looked, the stones often overbalanced and rolled back down to the ground. Alice's was the highest because she had the patience to wait and balance each stone carefully before she chose another one to lay on top. While Peter played with the rocks he tried to see if he could feel any magic in any of them. In the end, he picked on a very small pebble which had blue speckles on it that reminded him of Seraphina's lovely colour and he slipped it into his pocket. He didn't get a tell-tale prickle from it and he rather thought that Seraphina must have been teasing him.

His stomach was telling him it should be time to eat and he was pleased when his mum called them over for an early picnic lunch. As they ate they could see a couple of gannets diving for fish in the sea, leaving a fountain of water splashing upwards as they disappeared below the surface and then reappearing gobbling down a fish.

The shore was amazingly long and picturesque. After their picnic they explored the plentiful rock pools to see how many crabs and starfish they could find. There were often tiny fish darting about through the greenery at the bottom of the pools waiting to be released back into the sea when the tide came back in. Once they were finished doing that Peter and Alice started to run again across the beach, enjoying leaving their foot prints in the damp sand. Then they turned away from the sea to explore the sand dunes which were at the back of the beach. It was great fun.

"Shall we leave soon and see if we can find the scallop fisherman now?" dad called as he and their mum got closer to them.

When they finally arrived at Leverburgh the scallop diver, was sitting on his boat in the harbour shucking scallop shells. The shells were so big they were the size of a man's hand, the scallops inside them were huge. The fisherman made it look so easy popping open the shells and scooping the scallops out. He told them that he dived for them himself and Peter remembered reading somewhere that that could be a very dangerous occupation. There was a fishy smell in the air coming from the various fishing boats moored up close by.

Dad decided that two each would be plenty for them due to the scallops being so large and meaty and what's more he was determined he would shuck the eight scallops himself.

That evening there was lots of quiet swearing going on as Peter's dad realised that opening the scallops was not quite as easy as it had looked. The scallops were very strong and muscular and held tightly onto their shells. Eventually he managed to get them all open and cleaned and mum cooked some creamy mash, leeks and peas to go with them. They all agreed they were gorgeous and well worth all of dad's efforts in opening them. Peter and Alice were even allowed a small taste of the dry white wine that mum had chosen to go with them, but they rather thought that lemonade tasted better!

CHAPTER THIRTEEN

The next day Mr McMuran was quite surprised to see Peter again until his dad explained that Peter really enjoyed taking photographs of different birds and was always quite happy being on his own. Fortunately, Peter didn't seem to be expected to shake hands this time.

"Well, in that case I should have mentioned the small beach over that way," Mr McMuran said waving his hand in the opposite direction to where Spit was. "It does mean that long trek down some steps again but there is a rope handrail to hold on to and you can stop and watch the birds while you get your breath. It will be well worth your efforts to get down to it. You can go beachcombing – there is often bits of debris washed up on the stones." Peter did his best to look interested, although all he really wanted to do was to rush off and see if he could find Spit.

"Thank you, Mr McMuran," he said politely "I'll enjoy that. See you later dad." And he obediently headed off towards the direction of the beach. He thought that he'd better actually go down to it, just in case he was asked any questions about it later on. Once he found the steps he grabbed hold of the rope handrail which was attached to the side of the cliff face and clambered down towards the beach. There were many and although he started to count them he soon forgot where he had got to. He was more worried about how long it was going to take him to get back up them, particularly as he was still rather puffed from the hard climb up from the harbour.

Mr McMuran was quite right about the beach and before he had met Spit he'd have been content to spend a lot of time there watching the different birds flying across the sea and then up into their nests in the cliff. He saw many gannets and quite a few of the tiny lovely coloured puffins and counted at least five other species of seabirds. At one point, he looked up and saw a distant figure on the top of the cliff looking down at him. Peter waved and he could see a kilt swaying about in the breeze as the man waved back at him. Yep, he'd done the right thing in coming down here as it appeared that Mr McMuran was checking up on him. He wandered slowly about the beach to where it bent around a corner. Scanning the rocky cliff face above he gave a sigh of relief – he couldn't be seen from above so long as he kept close to the cliff face because the top of it overhung the beach. There were big boulders scattered around him which must have sheared off from the high walls of the cliff over the years, and he settled himself down amongst them, totally hidden from view as he waited very impatiently, and planned how he was going to get back up unseen.

Finally, he got up and crept slowly back the way he had come stopping at the sharp bend on the beach and using his binoculars to scan the area where Mr McMuran had been standing. Nothing there. Pressing himself very carefully against the rocky cliff face he slunk as fast as he could around the corner to the bottom of the steps and checked again. No, he was safe, he couldn't be seen here either unless someone was out at sea looking back at him, which wasn't the case. He began his long climb and was panting hard when he eventually got near to the top. He sat down for a brief spell to get his breath back and then eased himself up slowly to the top step and lay down to use his binoculars to scan the area around him. Nothing moved. He looked over to the house. Through one of the windows he was very pleased to see Mr McMuran with his back facing outwards bending over something Peter's dad was showing to him. Peter scampered from bush to bush keeping a sharp eye on the house in front of him. The dodgiest bit was where he would be in full view of what he assumed must be the office window so taking a big deep breath in he sprinted across the grassy area going straight to the wall next to the window. He stopped for a minute and peeked very carefully into the room. Both men were still engrossed in what they were looking at so he ducked down very low and crept past. Then he was off full pelt past some scraggy sheep which were grazing contentedly nearby and shot off in the direction of the entrance to the dome.

He burst through the barrier which gave with a small pop to find Spit tapping a dragon talon impatiently on the ground in front of him.

"Where have you been?" the little dragon asked, "I've been waiting forever! Archie let me know ages ago that he'd seen you so I knew to come here and wait."

"Sorry, Mr McMuran suggested I would like to go

and spend time on a beach somewhere else. I didn't want to, but its lucky I did because I saw him at the cliff top checking up on me."

"Well come on, then let's go and have some fun!" Spit started to bounce on his toes and sweep his tail about in the dust, his annoyance forgotten, and before he knew it Peter was coughing and spluttering and going very red in the face.

"Sorry!" Spit tried very hard to keep still but it was obviously a big effort for him.

As they set off Peter looked again up at the tall trees – it was so amazing that they were totally hidden from view if you looked at them from outside the magic bubble.

"What's that?" Peter pointed at something small, round and very green and luscious on the ground.

"A lady burger." Was the matter of fact answer.

All Peter could think of was something in a bun like a hamburger which was bizarre. It made him feel hungry and he could picture a lovely big beefburger with gherkins and mayonnaise and tomato sauce and all things yummy.

The lady burger had hundreds of legs that went all around its edge.

"It can't move far because its legs keep going in so many different directions so it has to rely on insects and small birds coming close to see if there is any food for them on it." Just as Spit said this a big long blue forked tongue flicked out of the top of the bright greenness and slurped up a fly that was overhead and before you knew it the tongue had gone. "Just like that! The tongue has a nasty barb in it and it goes in very deep and doesn't let go, so keep well clear of any lady burgers that you see."

"Are there many of them in here? I've never seen anything like it before."

"There are a few but they are easy to spot because they are so brightly coloured. Now that over there," Spit nodded with his snout to their left, "is a frillio and they are lovely to touch, so soft and gentle," and he walked over to the rose pink frillio, which looked like an anemone you found in the sea with its fronds waving about in the air, and pushed his big nose into it giggling as he did.

"It tickles," he said chuckling some more. "Come on you try!"

Peter was amused to see that Spit's snout and nostrils had gone rose pink like the frillio, but he still touched the waving fronds with his left hand and they felt very gentle, like someone stroking his hand. He wanted to keep his hand there because it was so soothing, but Spit was eager to get going again. Fortunately, his nose had gone back to its normal colour, however when Peter took his hand away from the frillio he saw that it too had changed to the rose pink hue, much like Spit's nose had been. The soothing feeling stayed with him until the colour disappeared.

Every now and then Spit would give a little dragon giggle and Peter learnt to brace himself as the dragon would leap at him to knock him down to the ground. Then they would play fight like children or puppies rolling over and over. Spit's sense of humour took some getting used to and after a time Peter realised he was quite grubby – he'd be in trouble when he got home. Spit also liked to practise breathing fire and anything close by would end up covered in wet snot. Peter tried to be encouraging about it even though it was very hard for him not to burst out laughing.

As he heard Spit giggle yet again, Peter prepared himself for another dragon onslaught but this time Spit told him to watch. He picked up a couple of pine cones in his maw, the name for his big mouth, and tossed them into the air in front of the pair of them. The seeds dropped out of the dry cones and began to tumble down to the ground and as they did hundreds of heads on long thin necks popped up, bobbing up and down, all at different times. No bodies appeared, just these small heads which had beaks on very long elegant necks. They were rather like flamingos without bodies snatching at the pine seeds and then disappearing back into their holes.

"I like doing this!" Spit said, "It makes me laugh." And he giggled naughtily again as he tossed another couple of pine cones into the air making the heads pop up and down like piano keys.

"What are they?"

"Swannees," was the answer.

There was a sharp caw caw near to them as Archie swept across in front of them and Spit used his tail to push Peter flat on the ground.

Peter peered over the long scaly tail and drew in a sudden deep breath, walking along not too far in front of them marched Mr McMuran, his purple kilt swaying with each step. Slider was almost skating along beside him.

"You know him?" Spit whispered into his ear.

"Yes, that's Mr McMuran, I believe he owns the island, but what is he doing here? He's let dad come here to interview him and look through some old papers in the house."

"He's the boss man."

"Where are they going?"

"There's a small building they go into, near where they leave my food." There was silence for a while as they watched Mr McMuran and Slider walk away from them.

"Wouldn't you like to be free?"

"Sometimes in my dreams I feel I am flying through the air, up in the clouds. It's just that I can't get out of here. Archie has described what it's like outside. I have tried many times to escape but I cannot break through the barrier."

"So, it's the same as being in a zoo or a cage." Peter thought "but no-one can visit, apart from me." He wasn't sure if Spit would understand what a zoo was.

They waited quietly together and that was when Peter felt it would be a good time to tell Spit about the dragon seer's caves and the pictures of Spit himself.

Spit was astounded. "I am shown in the dragon pictures? The elder dragons have seen me! Wow!!" and he gave one of his little dances as Peter tried desperately hard not to cough and splutter.

"So, if I could get to the caves then I might see where I came from and how I got here?"

"That's what McDragon says. Please stop that!" Peter said, choking amongst the cloud of dust. He had to be so careful not to be seen or heard as he desperately tried not to cough loudly.

As soon as the dust had settled again, "You would need to be able to fly Spit, to get to the caves because they are so high up in the sky but I am sure the other dragons would be happy to guide you."

Spit started to dance about again and Peter had to hold

his hand over his mouth because he had just glimpsed Mr McMuran and Slider talking heatedly as they marched back along the path. He watched carefully until they were out of sight.

"So, Mr McMuran is the man Slider reports to?"

The dragon nodded.

"I'm not sure I like him as I got an odd prickle on my neck when I shook hands with him." He then told Spit about how the mural had sent flames out of the picture as a warning.

Spit thought it was very funny that Peter had to shake hands when he met someone.

"Dragons would not do that!" he announced and as he said it he stopped. "What do you say when you shake hands Peter?"

"How do you do?"

Spit made a rumbling sound which Peter assumed was a chuckle and then Spit put out one big scaly front foot, talons sticking forward, and said, "How do you do Petersmith?"

Peter started to laugh and touched his hand to one of the talons giving it a shake as he did, and answered, "Very well thank you."

Then they started to roll about on the ground laughing as they both imagined fierce dragons going through the same formality. It was all very, very funny indeed.

It was so nice having a friend who made him laugh and, even better than that was to have one who was a dragon.

It wasn't long before they talked again about the dragon seer's cave. Peter was a little worried about his dad being with Mr McMuran but Spit reassured him, "I will ask Archie to keep an eye on your dad when he is here."

"That would be absolutely brilliant, but how would I know if dad was in trouble it's not like you can telephone me or you can get out of this, this er magic bubble!"

Spit had no idea what a telephone was but they both pondered on the problem for a while and then Peter looked at Spit gleefully, "Seraphina gave me one of her scales so I could contact her if I ever needed her," and he thrust his hand into his inside pocket and retrieved the soft scale to show Spit. "Maybe we could do the same with one of your chest scales." Spit touched the scale gently with his nose.

"It tingles me," he said giggling and did it again keeping his nose on the scale. Then he jumped back in amazement, "She spoke to me! She spoke to me! I've heard another dragon!" and he pressed his nose against the soft scale some more closing his eyes so he could commune with Seraphina.

A small tear trickled down his cheek when he finally took his head back.

"Seraphina called me by my name and said she was looking forward to meeting a brave dragon like me and she told me they would come up with a plan to rescue me so I could be free, as all dragons should be." He shivered with delight. "I told her I was going to give you one of my chest scales and she explained what I need to do. Oh, Petersmith, I am so very glad you came here! I can't explain just how happy it makes me feel!" and with that he started to prance about and the air filled with the scent of pine needles and dust along with dragon drool and sparks.

Peter started to cough.

"Sorry, Petersmith! I forget that it affects you so badly, but I am so very, very, excited!"

"I know Spit. I'm so glad you have finally spoken with another dragon. That is amazing! Now you know how to imbue the scale with your magic, shall we give it a try?"

Spit nodded his scaly head thoughtfully, "Oh yes, Petersmith. It would be nice to be able to talk to you when you are not here. It can get very lonely."

"I get lonely as well, even though I have my family."

Spit braced his neck and chest and indicated that Peter should pull off a scale from over his heart and Peter tugged hard at a small scale. It was a lot tougher than pulling out Seraphina's one but it gave way eventually.

"Now you need to touch my forehead with your snout, although I don't know what Seraphina did when she touched me."

"I do! I have to dragon burn you."

Spit bent his head forward closing his eyes to concentrate. Peter felt that tingle at the base of his neck as before as well as heat on his forehead until Spit pulled away.

"Well, we won't know if it worked until I'm gone from here I guess. Fingers and talons crossed!" and he held up his hand with his fingers curled inwards and held it out towards Spit who lifted one of his big feet and gently crashed a talon into Peter's knuckle.

CHAPTER FOURTEEN

Spit was hungry. Food, it seemed, was a big mess of smelly gunge piled up on the ground close to a small brick building. Nearby there was a handy log for Peter to sit on and eat his rather squashed sandwiches – all that rolling about and play fighting had not done them a lot of good. Spit's food consisted of mainly fish, which explained the smell. There was a worn pathway leading to the building which had a big padlock on a metal hasp attached to a stout looking door.

Spit spluttered as he gobbled his food, his table manners were non-existent. Peter grinned to himself, it was obvious that Spit had never met Peter's mum!

They studied the building as they ate. It seemed that Spit had no idea what was inside the building only that Mr McMuran and Slider visited it often. Peter could see a small window in the roof and he pondered on how he could get up and have a look inside. If he could use Spit as a ladder he might manage it.

Food eaten, they walked over to the building to try. It was definitely a tricky feat, particularly as Spit's neck scales were very sharp and pointed and Peter yelped a lot as he struggled to get a grip without hurting himself. When he reached the gutter he put a tentative foot on to it but it gave a little bit as he did. In the end he had to give up and slithered very ungracefully down onto the ground getting little cuts on his hands as he did.

As he landed on the ground he heard Archie giving his warning caws as he whizzed around the corner. The two friends shot into the nearby bushes to hide and peered through the big leaves just as Slider ghosted around the corner. He was holding a very large key which he inserted into the padlock and the door swung silently open.

Warmth came out of the small building wafting over to their hideaway but it was difficult to see what was inside due to Slider's bulk blocking the way. They could see him looking down and putting one of his hands out to touch something. He "Hmmmmed" to himself and then backed out of the doorway to lock the door behind him and slithered off back the way he had come.

Finally, Archie cawed to let them know the coast was clear.

Glancing around the big leafed bushes where they were hiding Peter could see that there were lots and lots of big white sticks bending up out of the pine needles on the ground. They all domed upwards to join another long white branch that was running along the top of them. It almost felt like being in a church the way the sticks joined together. Even Spit fitted comfortably inside because the space was so huge.

"Do you know what these are Spit?"

Spit shook his head so Peter ploughed through the

deep debris of leaves and small sticks along towards the end. Then he saw that the sticks came down and carried on along the ground quite a long way gradually getting smaller and smaller.

"Oh, I have a thought about this!" and he tapped on the nearest stick. It felt strong beneath his fist and not at all wooden like, it reminded him of something he'd seen on a school visit to the British Museum.

"Hmmm," he turned and walked back the way he had come and continued eventually coming to what looked like a humungous skull. Peter looked at this and then back at Spit and back again.

"Why are you looking at me like that?"

"Well, this looks much like the skeleton of something the same as you, but much much bigger, in fact more the size of McDragon. I really believe it is a dragon skeleton!" he announced. He marched back to where they had first been hiding and pointed up to the highest bones above them, "This is the rib cage that we are in and back there is the head and neck, and over there are the bones from the tail."

Spit looked totally dumbfounded. "A dragon! Is this what could happen to me if I stay here?"

"I wouldn't think so, after all they do feed you so you're not going to waste away."

The dragon was not happy at all. "But how did it come to be here? How will we find out?"

"I wonder how long it has been here." replied Peter thoughtfully. "Perhaps I should ask McDragon if there are any dragons that have gone missing in past years." Looking at his watch, he panicked a bit, "Oh dear, I mustn't be late, we need to hurry Spit!"

As Peter started forward he tripped and landed head first in a deep pile of brown smelly pine needles near the head end of the dragon skeleton. His left hand stretched out in front of him to stop his face hitting the ground. "Ow! That hurt my hand!" and shook his hand to try and relieve the pain. Once it felt a little recovered he used his other hand to burrow gingerly into the pile of leaves and find what it was that his hand had hit.

"Ooh er! What do you think this is Spit?" They both stared at a black slightly curved piece of something very hard. It was jagged at one end and then narrowed down at the other to a sharp point and down the middle there was a long white stripe. As Spit put out one large talon to touch it they both laughed, "So that is what it is!" It was just like a much bigger version of one of Spit's talons, although his were completely black.

"I'll put this in my rucksack to show McDragon! Oh no, I am going to be late getting back to dad!"

They set off at a run back to where Peter had come through the barrier; Archie flying as scout ahead of them. Again, Spit attempted to follow him through the barrier but he just bounced back further into the dome. He definitely could not get out if he wanted to. Archie, however, carried on and flew above Peter as he clambered up the very steep slope towards the log at the top. At one point, Peter stopped to get his breath. He clasped the small scale which was in his hand and it warmed to the touch. He closed his eyes and immediately a picture came into his head of a sad looking small dragon with tears running down his long dragony face.

"Spit, can you hear me?"

Spit immediately perked up and beamed happily and started to bounce on his feet and swish his tail back and forwards.

"Can you hear me Spit!" he shouted again at the scale.

"Oh, yes, how do you do Petersmith?!" and Peter could visualise Spit as he thrust out one of his front legs, pretending to shake hands.

"Very well, thank you Spit! I will let you know if I can come again to play tomorrow! Over and Out!"

"What does that mean?"

"Well in one of the wars that the humans had, they used speaker systems called walkie talkies and they used to finish their chat with "Over and Out!"

Peter could feel that Spit found this very amusing as he responded, "Over and Out Petersmith! Let me know if you can come back tomorrow. I will miss my small friend!"

CHAPTER FIFTEEN

"I'm sorry Peter but you cannot come with me tomorrow when I go back to the island. Mr McMuran suggested that you probably had done enough exploring, so I feel it would be rude to take you with me again."

"Oh, but dad, I really like it there. It is so different!"

"I'm sorry lad, I cannot take you if Mr McMuran doesn't want you there. He's been kind enough to let me look through some of his old papers which have not seen the light of day for a long time. So, that's an end to it I'm afraid because I don't want to offend him in any way. He's a very strange chap, but I can't quite put my finger on what it is that makes him different. For all that, he's been extremely helpful to me in my research, letting me interview him as well. You'll have to make do with exploring our beach until I have the time to take you somewhere else. If I have the opportunity I'll ask Mr McMuran if you can come with me when I return for my last visit."

Peter felt really low. How would he ever get to see his friend again? He gripped the scale in his pocket and when he was on his own in the boat he used it to tell Spit he wouldn't be able to see him tomorrow and why. Although it was disappointing not to be able to go to the island it was exciting to know he could still talk to the little dragon any time he wanted to.

When they got to the house the smell of baking greeted them, and Peter's eyes widened with delight when he saw his mum was just sliding something off a pan that was on top of the hob into a tea towel.

"What are those mum?"

"Scotch pancakes. Would you like some?"

"Yes please! Lots! I'm starving again. All that sea air I guess!"

Alice was sitting at the small table and laughed at him, "Peter you are becoming a pig! Be careful or you might go back to school fatter than Biffy!"

Peter snorted, "I can't help it if the Scottish air makes me hungry! My clothes still seem to feel the same and please can we forget about Biffy while we are here!"

"Ok," she agreed sheepishly. She knew how it upset him to hear Biffy's name.

"Why do you put them in the tea towel?" he asked his mum.

"To stop them drying out. Try a couple, just put some butter and jam on. No more than that as it will be dinner time soon."

They were delicious, and he licked his lips between each mouthful trying to stop the butter running down his chin. Then he watched mum take a steaming lardy cake out of the oven.

"That looks yummy mum!"

"Well it's so nice to have the time to do some proper

baking and we're getting through so much cake while we're here, or rather you are Peter! At home it's always a rush, what with work and keeping the house clean. We'll have it with tea tomorrow afternoon."

There wasn't any time to go down to talk to McDragon because Peter had to keep Alice company for a while before dinner. As a fine Scottish mist had settled in, they decided they would stay indoors and hope it would clear up before the next day. You could only just see the water lapping at the edge of the rocks from the house.

When Alice went off to her room, Peter used the time to download his photos onto the laptop which dad let him use. He made sure he backed them up onto a memory stick. When he looked at them though he noticed that the pictures he knew he'd taken of McDragon had not come out. He did, however, have some beautiful ones of the gannets diving into the bay which he was quite proud of and there was also the otter amongst them. He'd been careful not to take any when he and McDragon had been exploring because he didn't want to have to lie to his dad if he saw them and asked how he had got to these different places. He was very aware of his solemn promise to keep the dragons a secret.

After dinner the four of them played some board games which were stashed away in the lounge until Peter found himself yawning and excused himself to go off to bed. It had been a long day. Fortunately, his mum had not asked how his clothes had got so dirty or how he had got the small cuts on his hands.

The following morning he was woken by the front door closing softly as his dad went off to meet the boat to go to the island. Peter got up in a rush; he wanted to go and see McDragon. He sprinted down the beach with his left hand gripping a big red apple as he took a large bite out of it at the same time feeling in his pocket for the two dragon scales. He pulled up short – there was only one scale in his pocket!! He put the apple down on a nearby rock and started to search frantically through all of his pockets. It had to be there somewhere! He found some shells and the small stone which he had thought to show to Seraphina. There was a rather screwed up tissue, and his camera, but no scale! What was he going to do? How would he contact Spit? He went all hot and sweaty as he panicked, then taking a deep breath to calm himself he went through his pockets again slowly. Nothing. He tried to think where on earth he had put the scale. He could remember touching it on the boat when he had told Spit he could not go with his dad today, but he couldn't remember what he had done with it after that. He'd been feeling too miserable.

He sat down on the damp shingle and put his head in his hands. This was so awful and he felt sick with worry because he wasn't at all sure whether his dad would be safe on his own. If he needed help how would Spit let him know?

"A problem, Petersmith?" the big voice boomed in his head.

"Oh yes, McDragon, a very big one."

"Come and tell me all about it and let's see what we can do to sort it out." And Peter jumped up and started his journey to the dragon rocks again.

"Don't forget your apple Petersmith, you seem to get very hungry easily."

Peter went back for the apple, he didn't feel at all like eating it but McDragon was right, he did get hungry very quickly and he might need the apple to give him some energy.

"So, Petersmith, what is bothering you so very much?"

Peter launched into his tale about how his dad has said Mr McMuran didn't think Peter should go to the island again and how he had now lost Spit's scale so couldn't talk to him.

"That is strange Petersmith. I wonder what could be happening on the island for the man to stop you going back. Maybe he realised someone had been in the magical dome."

"McDragon, I am so worried about my dad as well, seeing that he appeared in the seer's pictures! Spit said Archie would keep an eye out for him and let me know if anything happened but without the scale he cannot get in touch with me!"

"Hmmm… Yes, I can see that you might worry, but as the boat's crew know he's on the island I think he should be quite safe. The other point is that you won't be able to get to the island to help him unless I take you there, but that is a bridge we will cross if we ever get to it."

Feeling a little better at that thought there was silence for a while and then Peter had an idea, "Of course there was one place I didn't look! In my jean's pocket. Mum took my clothes to wash because I can see my jacket is clean now, so maybe it fell out in the washing machine."

"In that case Petersmith, I think you should return to the house to see if it is there. You can come back to me anytime to let me know. I will be waiting for you. I need to prepare myself in case I am needed. My bones sense that we are getting closer to the time you will find the Pearl."

"But McDragon, I have no idea where it is!"

"You will know at some time, I am sure. It is written!" was the emphatic answer. "Now go back and see if you can find the clothes you wore yesterday."

"Yes sir!" Peter saluted at the big dragon and just before he started to scoot down the rocks back to the beach he smiled, "Thank you McDragon. If I hadn't got in such a panic I'd have had the sense to go back and look in my other clothes." And he was off, racing as fast as his legs, the rocks and seaweed would let him.

Drat, he had forgotten to tell McDragon about the dragon bones!

CHAPTER SIXTEEN

His mum was already in the kitchen when he got back as she sorted out some food for them.

"Porridge today," she announced. "And toast as well if you are very hungry, which you always seem to be in Scotland."

"Thanks mum," but all the time he was wondering how to bring up the subject of his dirty clothes from yesterday.

"By the way Peter, where did you get this? I've never seen anything like this before."

Peter nearly snatched it out of her hand but managed to stop himself. He wouldn't have got it back because he would have been in trouble for being rude.

"Oh, that's something I found on the island I went to with dad. I liked it because it is different." Well, he wasn't exactly lying because he didn't want to tell his mum a lie; that would have been wrong.

"It has a strange feel to it, almost tingly," she said holding it out to him.

"Really? That seems odd. Thank you mum for keeping it for me."

"Well, it fell out of your pocket so I thought it must be one of the finds you are saving for your collection." Fortunately, she was distracted at that point by the porridge nearly bubbling over and had to turn it down and by the time breakfast was over the scale was forgotten.

Peter gave a "Phew!" of relief once he left the house, so glad that Alice hadn't had a chance to see the scale because she would have been wanting to keep touching it and that would have totally confused Spit.

He was disappointed to see that McDragon was not on his rocks and he wondered why. He trudged along the small beach bending down to pick up small shells and toss them into the water. The good thing was he could have a think about all that had been going on. He was deep in thought when he felt winds battering him about the head and then the dragon landed neatly beside him.

"Wow, I didn't hear you coming until your wings pushed so much air at me."

"Good. I had to go and feed. When I am sleeping I am in a state much like hibernation so I don't need to, but now I must keep my energy up by making sure I eat regularly."

"Oh. I hadn't thought of that. But isn't it a bit dangerous at this time of day in case someone sees you?"

"Oh no, Petersmith, only humans who I allow to see me will do so. That is the dragon way."

"I found the scale," and he opened his hand to show McDragon. It felt very warm, much warmer than usual. "Oh, and I must tell you about the dragon skeleton we found!"

"A dragon skeleton? Are you sure?"

"It definitely looked the same shape and size as you

and like a very big version of Spit. We could both fit comfortably inside the rib cage. It must have been there quite a long time because the pine needles on the ground around it were very deep. Spit is scared that he will end up like that if he stays there." McDragon looked disturbed. Peter rummaged in his coat pocket and pulled out the talon. "I found this there as well and I thought you might want to see it."

"My, oh my! I only know one dragon that had talons with a mark like that. We wondered what had happened to her. Her name was Arletta." He looked sadly down at the talon. "So that is where she ended up! It must have been quite a long time ago if only a skeleton is left of her. I wonder how she got there?"

As McDragon was speaking, the small scale Peter was holding warmed up some more. He closed his eyes briefly and concentrated as a picture of Spit came into his head; a Spit that was bouncing about excitedly with Archie zooming round and round his head. It made Peter feel quite dizzy.

"How do you do Petersmith?"

"Very well, thank you Spit. Your scale heated up in my hand so I knew you wanted me."

The little dragon danced about some more and Peter was really pleased he was not beside him as it even made his vision of Spit foggy.

"Archie flew up to the window on the building we looked at yesterday!" Archie could be heard cawing and flying manically around Spit's head. "He says he could see what looked like a big oval stone on a bench with a warm red light shining on it."

99

"Oh, wow, a big stone! How big was it?"

There was a short silence and then the answer came back, "Well, Archie says it is about the size of your head. It has a large crack down it. What should we do? I don't think I can get in to rescue it and even if I could I wouldn't have anywhere to go with it as I can't get out of this bubble the way you do!"

"Let me ask McDragon, he is next to me now. Stay there, and stop bouncing about! What a brilliant idea asking Archie to go and look." Spit looked chuffed to be praised. Dragon magic was amazing. Fancy being able to get a picture in your head of the being you were speaking to!

Even though he could only hear one side of the conversation, McDragon looked very interested.

"Petersmith, what have they found?"

"Well, Archie flew up to peer through the window of the building which Slider visits a lot and he saw what looked like a big stone on a bench. We know something is being kept warm in there because when we watched Slider go into the building heat wafted out. I've seen chicken and duck eggs in an incubator when I've been on a visit with the school being kept warm like that to make them hatch!" gabbled Peter. "What should Spit do? If he somehow got into the building, he couldn't carry the Pearl nor can he get out of the magic bubble. The barrier repels him somehow. Also, Archie has told Spit that the Pearl has a crack in it!"

There was silence for a short while as McDragon looked very thoughtful as he pondered on the situation. Eventually he put his head next to Peter's and looked deep into his eyes, "Petersmith, tell him to do nothing for the moment and keep away from the building. Assuming it is the Pearl, we have to get to it before the dragonite comes out in case it should bond with Mr McMuran rather than a dragon. If it did that we would have a problem trying to get it away. I need to see Seraphina and Haribald immediately. To make matters worse we must keep an eye on the weather, it feels from the air that there is a bad storm coming this way. Be firm with your friend, we do not want anything bad to happen to him!" Peter nodded.

"Petersmith do you have Seraphina's scale with you? Are you able to contact her and ask her to meet me at the dragon seer's cave?"

"I'll do my best to speak to her McDragon."

"You are a good choice for dragon kin Petersmith! Now I must fly!"

The wind whistled around Peter's head as McDragon's wings beat in the air and he lifted straight off of the rocks heading upwards into the sky.

With Spit's scale tightly gripped in his hand, Peter closed his eyes and gave Spit the message. He explained that it was very important that Spit and Archie keep away from the building where they had seen the stone. Very important indeed! Also that McDragon had gone to have a pow wow with Seraphina and Haribald d'Ness.

"What's a pow wow?"

"It's a meeting where they can plan what should be done."

"OK, well I'll have to eat my food or else they'll think there is something wrong with me, but other than that I'll try to stay near where I first met you. Archie will keep an eye out in the meantime, just in case something happens," then Peter heard the dragon giggle, "Over and Out for now Petersmith!"

"Over and Out Spit! Keep safe. I would like to see you again in the flesh and not as a pile of dragon bones!"

CHAPTER SEVENTEEN

He had to fumble around in his pockets before he could find Seraphina's scale and, of course, it was in the last pocket he looked in. He gripped it firmly and thought of her. Nothing happened. "I must try harder," he thought and closed his fingers more securely around it. It was much larger than Spit's one so he had to transfer it to the hand that had four fingers and a thumb to get a better contact with the scale. He sat down on a nearby rock, closed his eyes and concentrated all of his thoughts on Seraphina.

"What are you doing Peter?" his sister's voice made him jump.

"Oh, I was just thinking about things. I wanted to see what it felt like if I closed my eyes and could just hear the sea and the birds calling to one another."

"Weirdo." Was the only answer he got to that but gave a sigh of relief when he saw that she'd transferred her attention to a pool over in the rocks and was scrambling across them to peer into it.

"Come and look at this crab, Peter!"

"OK, I'll be over in a minute. Just let me try my

experiment some more and see if the sounds are different over there." And he pointed to the other side of the rocks where he hoped to get more privacy.

"As I said, Weirdo!"

Peter ambled casually over to the other side of the dark grey rocks. They all had yellow on their tops, much like McDragon did. The scale warmed in his hand and out of nowhere a soft dragon voice spoke to him.

"Petersmith, do you need me!"

"Yes, Seraphina, although it is McDragon who needs you." Then he launched into a garbled tale of what had happened and how Spit thought they had found the Pearl and that it had a crack in it. Finally, he added breathlessly, "McDragon asked if you could meet him at the dragon seer's cave. He's gone to get Haribald d'Ness so you can all decide what should be done."

"Slow down Petersmith you are not making much sense. Tell me again but slowly."

A big deep breath calmed him and then he started over, trying not to rush at it this time.

"You think you have found my Pearl? I told you it was written that you would Petersmith and my dragon senses tell me that you have done just that!" He could feel her smile.

"Well, it was actually Archie who saw it, not me."

"But, Petersmith, if you had not been with Spit he would not have known about the Pearl. I will leave now Petersmith and wait for McDragon at the caves as he requested. Watch out for McDragon's return. Remember we will meet in dragon time so that your wait will seem really very quick to you."

He could hear her big wings unfolding and then the whoosh as she left wherever she was on her way to the dragon seer's cave.

"Seraphina!" he called out hoping she could hear, "Remember to look out for the squawkins!"

No answer.

"Who were you talking to Peter?" somehow Alice had managed to clamber over the rocks without him hearing her – he'd been concentrating so hard.

"You said I was a weirdo, so I was just proving I was. Let's go and see that crab you found. Race you!" and they scrambled and slid across the rocks while at the same time Peter made very sure he had the scale tucked safely away in his pocket.

They looked in the big pool where the crab was waving its claws at them. He was not that big really, only an inch or two across his shell. Then Peter suggested they went and looked inside the old shed, which was next to the house, to have a rummage there. She hadn't been in there before so Alice quite liked that idea. Peter at one point had stashed the length of rope that had the pulley on the end of it in there. It had seemed quite strong and the rope was lightweight and a good length. While Alice was occupied looking through other stuff that interested her he placed it quietly just outside the door. It might come in handy for something.

Alice soon got bored and wandered off into the house to see if their mum would let them have some of the lardy cake and it wasn't long before he followed her in. He could smell the lovely aroma of another fruit cake cooking as well. They had never had so much homemade cake in their whole lives before.

Mum was quite happy for them to try out the lardy cake and Peter asked if he could wrap his in some paper towel and eat it on the beach. The answer was a yes, and even more luckily, Alice opted to stay indoors with her mum. He found his pack and his water bottle, which he filled up.

"Oh, by the way Peter, you'll be pleased to know that dad rang to say he'll be picked up by the boat much earlier today as they are worried about a change in the weather. He'll be leaving around noon so we might be able to have an early dinner tonight."

"That's great mum. That would be good, you know how hungry I get." Naturally, he didn't mention that he knew the weather was going to turn because McDragon had already told him so.

Peter looked through the kitchen window and glared impatiently into the sky while his mum sliced him a big piece of lardy cake. There was nothing to see except for various seabirds. He put the warm cake into his bag.

"Mum, do you still have that old string bag that you keep in your handbag in case you get some unexpected shopping?"

"Yes. What made you think of that Peter?"

"Could I borrow it so I can keep it in my pocket just in case I find something I want to bring back from the beach?"

His mum sounded quite amused at that thought, but said yes and went and got it for him. He stuffed it in his jacket pocket and double checked in the other pocket to ensure that both his dragon scales were safely stowed away.

"Bye then! I'll see you in a little while!" and he gave his mum a peck on the cheek and just smiled at Alice as he left them in the kitchen, grabbing his coat on the way out.

He checked the sky again. Was that a large shape in the distance? It seemed to be heading towards the shore.

He nipped across to the shed and stashed the rope and pulley into his backpack. Then dashed across the beach to the dragon rocks.

McDragon's huge outline was approaching the rocks by the time Peter had reached them. Once he'd stopped he was panting from his run and had to bend over to try and recover his breath. As McDragon was landing he had the forethought to move the lardy cake from his backpack into his coat pocket and had a swig of water out of the bottle at the same time. The cake made a big bulge in his pocket but at least he knew he could get to it easily. He had a feeling he was going to need some sustenance quite soon.

CHAPTER EIGHTEEN

McDragon landed quite lightly next to him. "Spot on McDragon! That was the best landing yet!"

"Thank you laddie!" Peter looked at him expectantly and not very patiently.

"Well done Petersmith, for your message to Seraphina. She was there in perfect time to meet Haribald and myself and we took the opportunity to check the seer's pictures again. Of course, they had changed as we expected but, surprisingly only slightly, which wasn't very helpful. But never mind, we now have a plan!"

"What is to happen then? Mum says that the boat is going to pick up my dad early due to the weather."

"That's right Petersmith, the weather is going to make it a bit tough for flying, but Seraphina is desperate to get to the Pearl before the crack becomes any bigger or, even worse, it breaks open." McDragon put his head right down next to Peter's, "We will need you Petersmith, I'm afraid, and it may be dangerous!"

"That's fine McDragon, I am prepared. Will we be able to rescue Spit as well?"

"Yes, that's part of the plan, although that bit is a bit hazy at the moment. All three of us dragons will be going to the island with you so let's hope that nothing happens to any of us!"

"What will happen to Spit if we can get him out?"

"He will go with the Pearl to where Seraphina has found a safe hidey hole on a small island. Haribald will leave Loch Ness for the time being to be with her." He rumbled with laughter, "That will keep humans guessing even more when they visit the loch and there is no sighting of the Loch Ness monster for quite a while."

Even Peter smiled at that, despite the seriousness of their journey.

"Hold on a moment before you hop on board as I will need to warm you first!" He puffed hot air at the boy and Peter felt the dragon central heating warm him up nicely. "Now up you come, we have a good distance to fly and we need to get back before the bad weather really sets in. The other dragons are waiting for us and will join us as we pass the seer's cave. They stayed to check through the seer's pictures some more to see if we missed any clues in our haste that might help us."

As usual it was a bit tricky trying to clamber up to where the neck joined the body of the dragon particularly with his dodgy hand but he was soon settled into dragon riding position, the soft dragon scales gripping down on his knees to hold him tightly in place.

"You will have to be ready for any manoeuvres I may have to do if the squawkins attack us again. They were not anywhere near the seer's cave when we were there a while ago but I have a bad feeling about them. Be prepared to hold on very tightly." And with that the big dragon lifted himself into the air and firstly flew straight out to sea and then back towards where the seer's cave was across the land. Up and up and up they went but Peter still felt nicely warm and comfy and thought perhaps now would be a good time to eat some of the lardy cake to give him some much needed energy. As he broke some off he chewed on it thoughtfully and reviewed his situation which didn't look good at the moment. He hoped he would see his family again and realised with a shock that he hadn't said any proper goodbyes. He'd been in such a rush to get to McDragon. For all that, he felt he'd made the right decision, he would not be able to live with himself if he did not help the dragons or if anything bad happened to his friend, Spit.

The piece of lardy cake was very filling so he only ate half of it stuffing the rest into his pocket and feeling around for the scales as he did. He'd actually moved them into different pockets so if anything happened to one of them he would at least have the second scale.

"Shall I let Spit know what is happening McDragon?"

"Good thinking Petersmith. Tell him we'll let him know once we get near to the island. We'll have to fly low over the water and try and tuck in somewhere where we cannot be seen."

"The best place would probably be the beach where Mr McMuran suggested I explore before. I think he did that to keep me away from the hidden magic bubbledome. Then I'll have to clamber up all of those steps like I did before and carefully pass the house before I try to get in the dome at my usual place. That's around the other side of the island."

"Ok, Petersmith, we'll try that. It will be too obvious if I drop you off near your entrance in case we are spotted. As you have told me before, there is not anywhere to hide at that spot. We still have to think of a way to get Spit and the Pearl out of the bubble, but I will mull that over on our journey."

Peter sat comfortably in deep thought on top of the big dragon. It was absolutely amazing to be up in the air flying with the cold air brushing past his face while pushing his hair flat against his head. He wasn't at all chilly though as the lovely dragon heat kept him warm.

He felt around in the pocket he knew he had Spit's scale in and closed his hand around it without removing it from the pocket because it would be disastrous if the scale was gusted away in the wind. It warmed to his touch and he could see in his mind's eye Spit jumping around in excitement.

"How do you do Petersmith!" boomed into his head.

"Very well thank you Spit," he answered politely. "We are on our way to you now!"

Spit's voice in his head went all jiggley as he said, "Is McDragon bringing you here?!!"

"Yes, but I think you need to stand still Spit because it is getting more difficult to understand you!"

"OK! It's just that I can't believe that I am actually going to meet a real grown up dragon!"

"I know, I know. We're going to try and land on the little beach that Mr McMuran sent me to the other day when you thought I was very late, and then I will scoot as quickly as I can to where I usually come in and out."

"Are you going to try and get me out as well?" Spit asked sounding rather anxious.

111

"Yes, most definitely! We don't have a plan for that as yet but McDragon is working on it. Archie must come as well, of course, if he wants to."

He could see Spit leaping and twisting in the air and then the dragon disappeared as he was surrounded by a big dust cloud. Spit was coughing and spluttering so Peter was very, very pleased he wasn't there with him.

"Remember Spit, don't do anything but wait for me to come and make sure you keep yourself safe!"

"OK Petersmith. I'm hiding inside the dragon bones keeping watch but I'll start moving slowly over to our usual rendezvous soon. Archie is going to report back to me every now and then. They won't take any notice of him as he is always flying about."

"Good. It's lucky that McDragon seems to know where your island is as I have no idea how to get there. Over and Out Spit!"

"Over and... Oh, wait a minute Petersmith! Archie has just come to let me know that the Pearl is beginning to rock gently back and forwards! What does that mean?"

"Hold on, let me tell McDragon that!" Peter relayed the conversation to McDragon who began to beat his wings much harder as he replied.

"That is unexpected! It means that it is very close to hatching. We must go faster! This will be our only chance to save the dragonite. Now I must concentrate and not speak unless I have to Petersmith. It is going to be a tough flight."

Peter felt them go faster and faster and higher and higher as he told Spit what McDragon had said about the Pearl and what it meant if it hatched before they had rescued it.

Peter could almost feel Spit blowing himself up tall and big and important as he announced, "In that case Petersmith, we must make sure that I am near the Pearl when it hatches. It must bond with me and NOT Mr McMuran!"

"Wow, Spit, you are fantastic! You should be proud of yourself to take that on!"

As Peter finished his sentence he felt McDragon swerve to the left and Peter realised they were about to be under attack from two red squawkins. He held on to the neck scales in front of him very tightly with one hand. He could see that one squawkin was diving from above and the other one was now coming up from underneath them. Their yellow eyes looked evil.

"I must go Spit, Over and Out. We are under attack! I hope we see you soon!"

"Over and out Petersmith. Be careful!"

Peter released his hold on the scale in his pocket as he tried very hard not to feel afraid, but it was incredibly difficult not to imagine himself falling from the dragon's back and spiralling down and down towards the rocks below.

"I must be brave! I am dragon kin!"

They were nearing the dragon seer's cave but it looked unlikely that they would be able to take refuge there because, out of nowhere, another squawkin was coming from behind.

"Look out McDragon, there's another squawkin on your tail!" The third squawkin opened its huge maw and snapped as McDragon flung his tail from side to side trying to avoid it. The other two squawkins attacked at the same time, their dangerous talons ripping holes in McDragon who was fighting for his life. Peter could see deep cuts on the big dragon's side. Dragon blood was oozing out of the gouges. Peter tried to keep as low as he could, he remembered McDragon saying that if the talons caught him he would probably die. What could he do! He reached behind him and brought his backpack further to his front so he could rummage about in it. It was a tricky thing to do as they ducked and dived. He finally managed to get a hand on the rope and pulley and he dragged it out of the bag to swing it in a circle above his head again and again, just like the cowboys did with a lasso and he let it out longer so that it banged the nearest squawkin on the nose. The squawkin screeched in pain and swung away for a few moments, but then still screaming it started to race towards McDragon again but that had given the dragon a moment to gather himself together again.

Then it came to Peter! He fumbled about in his pocket for Seraphina's scale as he swayed from side to side. It was lucky he was tightly held down by the dragon scales. He ducked to avoid the beast that was diving from left to right.

He clutched the big scale tightly in his hand shouting as he did, "Seraphina! Seraphina! Help us please! We are being attacked!"

He didn't think that he'd managed to contact her but he could feel the scale was gradually warming in his hand.

"Seraphina! We need you! McDragon is under attack!"

Silence.

"Seraphina! Help!!" A squawkin rammed into McDragon and pushed him totally off course and he began to spiral down and down. Peter was pushed so he was almost flat on his back while still clasping the rope in his crippled hand. They twisted and turned as if they were on a rollercoaster ride and Peter could feel the enormous dragon fighting the airwaves as his big wings whooshed harder and harder. Little by little he appeared to be pulling them out of their dive. Suddenly a squawkin appeared to twist past them on their left hand side, screaming its horrible sound, looking like a huge cricket ball being turned and turned in the air, totally out of control, followed by a ball of flame. Then another squawkin screamed past. Finally, the last one too disappeared downwards towards the ground. Peter had to clutch his hands to his head to shut out the terrible screeching that was vibrating around his brain.

He smiled and relaxed as he saw that Seraphina was flying alongside them. Haribald came up on the other side of McDragon.

"Thank you both! Thank you so much!" Peter called to them.

The dragons nodded at him and then Seraphina flew closer to McDragon and touched her mouth to one of the cuts on his side. There was a hissing sound and steam rose up towards Peter and he saw the biggest gash heal up. She continued to fly right beside them as she healed other wounds and once that side was mended Haribald did the same on his side.

"Thank you, Seraphina and Haribald d'Ness," said McDragon breathlessly. "Well done to you too, Petersmith, it gave me a moment to try and recover when you used the rope like that."

Peter sat up proudly.

"Peter if you had not used the scale it could have been a different story," Seraphina told him. "It could be the two of you hurtling towards the rocks below, not the squawkins. Sadly, I do not think that they'll actually crash into the rocks, they are too agile for that but it will give us a little time to get away."

The dragons conferred making sure that Peter could hear them as they discussed the pictures in the dragon seer's cave. It seemed that there was a drawing which showed two dragons each side of a hole in the side of the magic dome. They were both gripping the sides of the dome with their talons where the gap was making it like a doorway. Petersmith was there as well. None of them had noticed this drawing before so it must be a new addition.

"That is what we must try and do so that Spit can get out!" she announced, "But it will be very hard to do it without being noticed. The two dragons that are in the picture seem to be McDragon and Haribald, I am nowhere to be seen."

They were finally passing the giant gannet stacks and without any agreement all started to fly downwards to keep low over the sea. A small white boat was bouncing about on the waves beneath them and as they flew down closer to it Peter was happy to notice that his dad was standing on the foredeck wearing a yellow life jacket; there was no point waving at him because his dad wouldn't be able to see the dragons passing above them. The boat rocked about a little more as the air flow from three pairs of dragon wings made the sea even choppier. Looking up Peter could see dark clouds beginning to loom above them. The weather was definitely on the turn.

CHAPTER NINETEEN

With the island finally on the horizon they began to rise using the air currents to help them. It had been a very blowy and bumpy flight. The wind had risen and pushed against them. The sea was very rough below them with lots of white bursting on the crests of the waves. Peter was so pleased he was not on the boat or else he might have done an Alice over the side.

The magic dome was still invisible from up here and he mentioned that to McDragon.

"I think it has been covered by very special magic," he replied. "After we drop you off we'll fly above you so that we can see where you go into the bubbledome where we will wait for you to let Seraphina know when you are on your way out. At that time, we will hover as close as we can to where you should exit, landing only at the last minute for safety. We need to do everything we can so we do not end up as a pile of bones like poor Arletta did."

"Sounds like a good plan to me. I'll let Spit know we're close." And he felt for the small scale. It wasn't there! He felt carefully around in each of his other pockets but there was no sign of it and he started to panic.

"Breathe deeply," he told himself trying to slow his heart down which was charging along nineteen to the dozen. "Try again!" He did another very slow search for it but it wasn't there.

"Oh dear, McDragon, the scale isn't in the pocket I left it in nor is it in any of the other pockets! It must have been dislodged when the squawkins attacked us."

"Never mind Petersmith, you will have to improvise as best you can. Maybe Archie is out looking for you but if not you will just have to try and find Spit inside the magic dome. You can do this! It is written!"

Peter gave a sigh, "Well, I can't give up now we are so close but it is going to make matters much more difficult because I am not sure of the way to the building. I rather think that Archie will be keeping an eye on the Pearl so he won't be about." His voice tailed off. "You are right, McDragon, I can do this task!" He didn't add that the thought of being on his own in the dome scared him witless.

"Remember you are dragon kin Petersmith," Seraphina had been listening to their conversation. "We have faith in you!"

Haribald also added his encouragement from where he was on the other side of McDragon. They had been flying as if they were the Red Arrows, one at the head of the formation and two just a little way back, each of them either side of McDragon but slightly back to be in line with his wings. All it needed was some red, blue and white smoke to trail behind each of them.

On reaching the island they hugged the coastline as Peter guided them towards the little beach. He could feel his heart beating in his chest and he was trying very hard not to shake with fear. He was dragon kin and he was sure dragons did not tremble when they were scared. He thought of his mum, dad and Alice and wished and hoped that he would see them again. If he ever managed to get back to the cottage he would give each of them a very, very big hug, even Alice!

The stones on the beach rattled and crashed against one another as McDragon landed, leaving the other dragons hovering above the rough sea. There was not enough room on the beach for all three big dragons. They had flown in at a very low angle so that they could not be seen from the house. None of them was at all certain that their own dragon magic would hide them from Mr McMuran or Slider if they were spotted. The beach was quite protected from the wind because of the nearby cliffs, which made the landing a little easier.

"I need to go up there and get past the house without being seen," Peter told McDragon as he pointed at the steps. "Then I have to cross over to the other side of the island."

McDragon told him the three dragons would go high in the sky to watch over the island and see where he entered the dome and then hover up there as they had agreed.

"You do have Seraphina's scale, don't you Petersmith?"

Peter checked. "Yes, it's here safely." He also made sure that he'd stowed away the rope and pulley and the string bag inside his haversack. Then trying to look very brave, with a little wave at McDragon, he started off towards the rocky steps and grabbed the rope handrail to help himself balance as he went up. He heard, rather than saw, McDragon lift up off of the beach. There was a great pulse of air displaced by his huge expanse of wings as well as a loud crunching of the stones banging against one another. It was lucky that the wind was making enough noise to hide his departure.

Peter carried on up the steep steps and stopped to draw in a big breath half way up. He could smell the sea and the seaweed which almost made it seem rather nice and normal. Finally reaching the top, he felt the high wind battering him and nearly knocking him over the side of the cliff so he dropped himself down as low as he could, then tried to move like he'd seen the SAS did in films, in short spurts tucking down behind one bush and then another. Before he reached the house he slowed down and peered out from behind an evergreen shrub so he could check that no-one was looking out of any of the windows. Pulling his binoculars out of his pocket and holding them up to his eyes he studied each window carefully. It all seemed quiet until he glimpsed a movement in the study. Oh no! The man stood up and peered down at the desk. It was Mr McMuran and he was reading through something on the desk in front of him. Should Peter take the risk and run now or should he wait? His heart was pounding with fear and he had to wipe sweat from his brow while he considered his dilemma. This was going to be one of the most dangerous parts of the whole exercise so he had to be sure.

Mr McMuran turned to stare at what seemed to be a map which hung on the wall behind the desk and was moving his finger across it as if to mark out a route. This was it! Peter took his life in his hands and set off in a low run towards the house keeping a close eye on the man in the study as he did. At that very moment, Mr McMuran turned away from the map and Peter threw himself down flat on the ground next to some rather tall scrubby plants. Peering through them he could see the man looking through the window as if a movement had caught his eye but suddenly there was a tweeting sound and a bird flew out of a nearby bush. Mr McMuran turned his head to track its flight. Peter waited. It was very hard to stay still as his whole being wanted to escape, but his gut feeling was that he shouldn't move a muscle so he remained like a statue.

Minutes passed and the wind whistled around him. It felt like he had been there an absolute age when at long last the kilted man turned towards the study door and Peter was off, as fast as his legs could carry him, out of view of the house and on and on across the grass and then round to the other side of the island. He finally came to a halt next to the log he had fallen from when he had first tumbled against the dome. He couldn't go on until he had caught his breath. It seems aeons ago when he had first been here. Shame he'd lost the scale so he couldn't get hold of Spit. He looked up high above him and could see the three specs which would be the dragons circling up near the clouds, and he waved frantically at them. One of them tipped sideways as if to acknowledge him and then flattened out again.

Gradually his breathing slowed down and he wiped the sweat from his forehead with his arm.

Time to go in. He checked that he had everything at the ready. His pack was safely on his back.

Down the slope until he felt the gentle pop of the magic wall and the tingle as he walked through it. There was no wind in here to blow him about – it was very silent and creepy. He stopped to get his bearings and let his eyes adjust to the gloom. It smelt just as musty as before, with the scent of pine needles and animal poo. Not the nicest smell in the world.

CHAPTER TWENTY

The mamothias were in their original positions, like statues facing one another, so he gave them a wide berth and edged very carefully past them. He didn't want to be chased like he had before.

There was no sign of Archie or Spit but he couldn't hear anything big moving about close by, which was a bonus. He spotted the ladyburger and saw her flick out her blue forked tongue and spear a passing fly which made him think he was going in the right direction.

A bit further on was the frillio and despite his haste he couldn't resist stopping to push his bad hand into the waving fronds relishing the soothing feeling it gave. It made the whole of him feel so much calmer too.

Now he needed to look out for the swannees, but he couldn't see any evidence of them at all. He looked behind him. Maybe he was going the wrong way but how could he tell? It was so confusing in here and the animal smell was quite smothering. He needed Spit more than ever. Another few steps forward and he stopped again. Perhaps there was a way to check where he was going and he stooped down and picked up a handful of pine cones to toss them high in the air just in front of him. Nothing happened.

He threw some more to his right but again no movement anywhere. Behind him he thought he could hear something big moving so he knew he needed to get going as soon as possible and with a panicky movement he threw more cones down to his left. Pop, pop, pop and up popped the heads and long necks of the swannees. Thank goodness. He was on the right track. He checked behind him and then set off again in the direction he thought they'd gone in before.

He could hear a thump, thump, thump and stopped to listen where it was coming from. It was a very regular beat and then he realised, silly boy, it was his heart which was thundering along nineteen to the dozen.

His feet crunched on the pine needles as he moved off towards where he thought the Pearl was.

A kind of slithery sound came from in front of him and he threw himself flat down on the ground, keeping his face as low down as he could. Peeking through his eyelashes he spotted Slider, gliding along heading towards the small building. It was a relief in a way, because it meant he wasn't lost anymore.

"Whew! That was close!"

Once Slider had disappeared into the building Peter picked himself up and crept across to Arletta's dragon bones. As he finally stepped into the great cathedral of her chest he was slapped hard onto the floor of dirty pine needles and leaves.

"What the…! Oh, Spit!"

The Spit that had flattened him was a pitiful sight, covered in dirt, pine needles and dragon blood.

"What happened to you Spit?" whispered Peter.

"I was trying to get close to where I usually eat and the mamothias came out of nowhere and bundled me about. They bit me and it hurts lots! I usually manage to keep out of their way. I don't know what's upset them!"

"Have you tried using your drool on the cuts? That should help seal them up."

"Really, I didn't know that!" And with no more ado, Spit dribbled on one of his cuts. There was a hissing sound and he stared in amazement as he saw the gash begin to heal.

"How did you know that would happen Petersmith?"

"McDragon had some wounds he had to mend. Amazing isn't it? Shame it doesn't work on humans! I'm sorry I couldn't let you know I was here Spit, but I lost your scale when some squawkins attacked us earlier."

As Spit continued rendering his first aid, Peter watched the building intently. He could see Slider inside just looking down at what must be the Pearl, then he nodded and came out hurriedly and rushed off away from them.

"I think we might need to try and rescue the Pearl urgently, Spit. It looks like Slider is in a rush so I guess he will be bringing Mr McMuran here."

They crept out of the dome of dragon bones and over to the building.

"If you can help me back onto the roof, I seem to remember I saw a big nail sticking up near the top and I have a rope I can hook over it and pull myself up. But where is Archie? I rather think he may have to go in through the window and help me from inside."

Spit looked up into the air and then issued a strange

125

whistling noise loudly through his nostrils twice. There was a fluttering and the big black bird came from the direction of where the swannees were.

"There he is! He went off to see whether he could spot you and the dragons flying over the sea."

Archie pecked gently at Peter's hair which Peter assumed was supposed to be a friendly hello gesture.

"Archie, if I climb on Spit I may be able to get onto the roof near that window. Then I can try and break it. Do you think that if I do, I could help you go in through the window? I'm too big to get through the gap and we don't have time to take tiles off the roof to make a hole."

Archie cawed and Peter guessed that meant yes.

He took the blue rope out of his pack and looped it around his shoulder. It was very hard trying to scramble up onto the roof from Spit's back and he had to make sure he did not step on the wobbly guttering because he knew from his previous attempt that it would not hold his weight. Spit had to twist his neck and head around and then push him very hard with his snout to hold him in position. At the same time, Peter tossed the rope which he had looped up to try and lasso the big nail which he could see sticking up in the air.

He missed.

Tried again.

And missed.

Spit was wobbling about despite making a huge effort to keep Peter in place.

It was getting a little scary because they knew they might not have much time before Mr McMuran and Slider returned. With a gentle whoosh of wings Archie flew over and picked up a loop of the rope in his big beak dropping it over the nail.

"Thank you! Why didn't I think of that?"

Peter clutched on both sides of the rope which was now pulling tightly against the nail and then he tugged and tugged, dragging himself inch by inch up the side of the roof. It was a tricky business, particularly as his dodgy hand couldn't grip as well as the good one but at least he didn't need to work out how to use the pulley.

Something cracked loudly as a couple of tiles broke beneath him but he was now determined to finish this and finally… puffing and panting managed to sit with one leg either side of the pitched roof.

Holding tightly on to the rope he coiled it up again and wrapping some of it around his hand to protect it he smashed down on the glass using the pulley as a hammer. Nothing happened. He tried again and again. It took a couple of blows but finally there was a cracking sound and wrapping the rope more tightly around his hand he banged away at the broken shards of glass. Some of it clattered down beside the Pearl.

He peered down through the gap.

"Wow! That is what a dragon's Pearl looks like!"

As Archie had previously reported, there was a big crack down one side of the Pearl but it was not that deep yet. The Pearl, however, was rocking very slightly from side to side as if whatever was inside wanted to get out.

Peter tied the rope securely around the handle of his mum's string bag at the same time calling to Archie, who was hopping about impatiently at the other end of the ridged roof.

"Do you think if I lower this bag down to the Pearl and we try and keep it open, you could somehow try and nudge the Pearl into the bag please?" Archie cawed his acceptance and hopped onto Peter's hand. Holding the big bird gently he fed him through the broken window. Archie couldn't have done it on his own as his wings would have got in the way. Once through the gap Archie flew down.

Peter lowered the string back down onto the bench next to the Pearl, however it was soon very obvious that it was an impossibility for Archie to push the Pearl into the bag which Peter was trying to hold open by raising the rope attached to one side gently.

"Spit!" he called over his shoulder down to the waiting dragon. "Can you find a very long stick, maybe the length of your tail, please? I might be able use it to nudge the Pearl into the bag."

Spit bustled off importantly into the undergrowth. While he was gone Peter explained to Archie what he hoped to do.

There was a loud cracking sound to their left and Peter was shocked to see Spit return dragging one of the smaller rib bones from the dragon skeleton with him. Even a small bone was quite long and it still had a vertebrae at one end of it, rather like a golf club.

With a lot of manoeuvring, Spit managed to transfer the end of the bone up to Peter. It was an awkward job and it made Spit snort a lot. The boy fed the bone through the broken window and asked Archie to try and tug one side of the bag closer to the bottom of the Pearl. Once that was done Peter wrapped the rope around his waist to try and keep the bag open and then he used the vertebrae end of the bone to nudge the Pearl very, very gingerly closer and closer to the edge of the bag. It was a very tricky business. The heat lamp in the room made it hot work for the two of them and Peter soon had sweat pouring off of his brow. Every now and then the crow would tug at the mouth of the bag to try and open it out more. Peter just kept tap tapping with the dragon bone. He hoped the Pearl would not crack wide open, that would be a disaster and what would be even worse was if it fell off the bench onto the ground.

At last they got the Pearl into position at the very edge of the opening of Peter's mum's string bag. Spit called up to say he was going to keep guard over the route that he thought Slider and Mr McMuran would probably use.

"Steady does it!" Peter muttered to Archie and he tapped the Pearl a little more forcibly with the knobbly end of the dragon bone, much like a golfer would.

Peter kept concentrating, trying hard not to panic when he heard large animal footsteps rushing towards them. It was crucial now that he did not nudge the Pearl too hard.

"Petersmith, they come! Hurry!" called Spit skidding to a halt by the side of the building.

With a last gentle tap, the white dragon bone prodded the Pearl into the mouth of the bag.

"Phew!! Can you hook the string over the end of this big bone please Archie and I will lever it up towards me?"

Slowly, but surely, the bag with the heavy dragon egg in it was raised up into the air. Peter could feel the vibration of the egg through the bone he was holding. Finally, he was at last able to take hold of the bag itself and tug it through the window.

"Petersmith, they are nearly in sight!!"

"Can you do anything to delay them Spit? Bump into them or something!"

Spit shot off towards the bushes again.

Peter looked down.

"Archie fly up and I will lift you out!"

The bird tipped his head to one side and flew upwards and pecked at Peter's hand.

"Ow, why did you do that?!"

The bird pecked again and then flew back down to the bench and stared beadily at the door.

"Okay I get it, you plan on flying out of the door when it opens to create a diversion!"

He pulled the dragon bone through the smashed window and threw it down into the nearby bushes.

Peter could hear someone not too far away shouting, "That clumsy Wee Spittle!" and he guessed that Spit had barged into Slider and Mr McMuran. There wasn't time for him to use the rope to lever himself down the roof so he swung his leg over the ridge and slithered down the tiles. More of them cracked under his weight. He clutched the warm Pearl and bag tightly against his chest with his bad hand and used the good one and his feet to brace himself so that he did not crash down to the ground.

He heard, rather than saw, Mr McMuran and Slider as they crunched up to the door but there was no sign of Spit with them. He dropped from the edge of the roof as silently as he could and hoped the pine needles below would cushion his fall. One of his legs gave way as he landed and he felt pain shoot up it but he ignored it, his focus totally on keeping the Pearl safe. The rope slithered down from the roof and landed next to him and he gathered it up quickly looping it over his shoulder and untying it from the bag. It might come in handy for something maybe.

The big key made a grinding sound in the lock and Peter panted quietly as he heaved the string bag with the Pearl inside it into both arms and then dashed into the undergrowth next to the building. There was a rustling noise and Spit came up beside him.

CHAPTER TWENTY ONE

As the door creaked open Archie gave an enormous caw which was followed by a lot of shouting from inside the building.

"You stupid bird!! How did you get in here?!" Then there was another raucous caw and a loud bang and silence. No sound at all and no bird in sight either.

Spit and Peter looked at one another, "Should we do something to help Archie?"

Spit looked down at the dragon egg and then back in the direction where Archie was and shook his head sadly.

"I don't think we will be able to do anything to save him. He would want us to continue with the plan to rescue the Pearl or else our efforts will be wasted." With tears running down his long cheeks he pushed Peter with his big snout, "Run! Fast!" Peter found himself fighting not to cry. He was hobbling a bit because his leg still hurt from the fall but they were moving as quickly as a small dragon and a boy could go. The weight of the Pearl made it quite hard.

"I hope you know the way Spit, because I don't!"

"Where's that idiot dragon, Wee Spittle?" shouted Mr McMuran, his voice getting louder as he came out of the building, "He's at the bottom of this! Find him! We need that egg!"

Looking over his shoulder Peter could just see Slider coming out of the doorway followed closely by Mr McMuran as they set off after the dragon.

Spit did a sharp right turn heading towards the swannees and as he thumped along on his stubby legs he snatched up some pine cones in his mouth and, once they had run past the place where the swannees were, he tossed the cones into the air behind him. The long swannee necks and heads immediately popped up above the ground and Mr McMuran and Slider stumbled to a halt as they crashed into them.

"You! How did you get here?!" the kilted man shouted as he caught a glimpse of Peter dodging through the pine trunks.

"I knew there was something about you – you didn't feel right!" and as Peter glanced behind them he saw McMuran put his hand up one sleeve and pull out a wand which he pointed straight at him.

Sparks flew out of the end of it heading directly at him and he threw himself behind a tree yelping as the flames hit his good hand which he'd flung out to balance himself. Still he managed to keep the string bag clutched safely against his chest. He screamed out in pain again as a burning feeling surged up his arm. He could smell that his hair had been singed as well.

"He's a magician Spit! What can we do?"

"You keep going, you know the way now? I will try and

hold him off a bit. Petersmith, promise me you will carry on even if something happens to me! The Pearl is more important than anything. Swear you will, please!"

"Spit, please be careful; you are very important too but I promise you I'll continue no matter what happens! The dragons will be waiting for us!"

Spit touched his nose to Peter's very gently. It was like a kiss from a dragon and Peter gave him a watery smile back and stroked his neck.

"Quickly now Peter, take another one of my scales! We may need it!" Checking behind them Peter could see that McMuran and Slider were still struggling to get past the swannees which were continuing their bobbing up and down dance, a sea of spikes.

Another small scale was wrestled with and taken from over the dragon's heart and the same performance of the nose to Peter's head took place very quickly. The scale was secreted immediately in to Peter's inside pocket and then they were off in separate directions. Spit was going to circle around the back of the magician so Peter went the other way using the frillio, which he saw was in front of him, as a marker. He clutched his poor burnt hand against the still warm vibrating Pearl.

Another crack sounded behind him and he ducked down low to avoid the sheet of flame that was coming towards him. Because he was holding the Pearl against his chest he couldn't use his hands to balance himself and he fell head first down towards the ground just managing to twist at the last minute so that the Pearl did not hit the ground beneath him. When he opened his eyes, he was surprised to find that the frillio was immediately next to his face. Without thinking he plunged his painful burnt hand into its centre. The relief was amazing – his hand stopped throbbing and burning and he felt it cooling. He knew he only had a moment or two to do this, but it was absolute bliss for that short time. When he pulled it out of the lovely pink thing, as before his hand was quite pink but that was all that was wrong with it, the pain had gone from his hand and arm. Quite amazing!

There was silence around him for a moment or two. McMuran wasn't in view or Slider, so he crept along keeping very low and hid behind a nearby tree trunk which was quite wide surprisingly for a pine tree. It was lucky he was small because he couldn't be seen as he pressed himself against its rough bark, inhaling a strong smell of pine. He hunkered down to try and see what Spit was doing. The dragon was nowhere in sight. He scanned the area again, listening carefully to see if he could judge where they were.

The bushes in the direction he had just come from moved slightly and he saw Spit very briefly with a very fierce look on his face. Then Peter spotted McMuran (he had abandoned the Mr as he didn't feel the magician deserved that title). Slider was beside him. The pair had their backs to his friend as they scanned the area around them. Spit appeared to breathe in deeply and out of nowhere a lot of spittle issued from his mouth and then… fire! Flames started licking at the pine needles on the ground around McMuran!

"Well done Spit, what a time to manage to do that!" shouted Peter as he set off at a fast pace towards the edge of the magic dome. He was puffing and panting with the effort.

There was a loud crack and looking over his shoulder Peter was shocked to see that McMuran was pointing his wand at the little dragon, who had crumpled unmoving to the ground surrounded by a ring of fire! He desperately wanted to rush back and help but he had promised Spit that he wouldn't do that under any circumstances, so he carried on, tears streaming down his face. It seemed that his two new friends might both be dead, Spit certainly looked like it from the way he had collapsed.

As he sprinted onwards Peter took out the big dragon scale from inside his pocket and grasped it. It warmed to his touch and he shouted at Seraphina so the dragons would know that he was close to the perimeter of the dome. He put it back in his pocket and then still sobbing and running he somehow managed to take out the small scale which Spit had just given him.

The scale remained cold and lifeless in his palm.

"Spit!!! Spit!!! Please Spit hear me!"

There was no response and no answering warmth.

He continued clutching the scale and calling as he ran on towards where he knew the older dragons would be waiting. In his distress he forgot to check where he was going and yelled out in fright! The mamothias were almost upon him, looking very ugly and gnashing what he assumed were their teeth at him while trying to trap him between them. He came to an abrupt halt and drew in a very deep and angry breath – nothing was going to stop him in his quest to save the Pearl … certainly not two mamothias!!! He owed it to Spit and Archie! He ploughed forward very fast and surprised himself to find he could dodge about as if he was playing rugby, something he had never ever been any good at, the Pearl clasped tightly to his chest where he could feel it moving gently about.

"You will not get me!" he shouted and then to his horror he saw that McMuran was not far behind the mamothias with Slider following on with an ugly grin on his face. Peter could see flames were eating up the ground behind them.

Thrusting Spit's scale deeply into his pocket and making sure he had a firm grip on the Pearl in one hand, he gripped to the end of the rope with the one. Amazingly it was still looped over his shoulder and he stopped abruptly to turn to face his attackers. As he had done when he hit the squawkin, he used his good hand to swing the rope round and round above his head. The pulley whooshed as it got faster and faster and faster. He let the rope slip through his fingers so it got longer and longer as the pulley's weight pulled on it. When he saw McMuran reach for his wand he shouted loudly, "This is for Spit and the dragons!" Peter let go of the rope. Bullseye! The magician was felled in one foul swoop, dropping like a stone to the ground as the pulley knocked him on his head, his wand flying out of his hand. Slider had to stop when he almost tripped over the wizard. The mamothias spun around and promptly set upon him, they obviously felt they did not owe him any allegiance, he was as good a bait as anyone else.

Peter ran. Thankfully the edge of the bubble dome was in sight and it was a great relief when he flung himself through the barrier. It popped gently, a bit like a little burp and he was out… out in the fresh sea air where a gale was blowing. He looked back but the magic dome was like a shield and he couldn't see anything through it.

The three dragons were waiting impatiently for him at the top of the steep slope, their tails being buffeted by the rising wind.

Peter clambered up to the top and held out the Pearl in its string bag to Seraphina. She touched him gently on the forehead and then put her snout against the Pearl. Haribald did the same. They both hummed for a brief moment.

"I'm sorry but I need to get this little Pearl back to a place of safety as soon as possible! It is not far from hatching." Seraphina announced and taking the bag containing the Pearl in her maw without any more ado she spread her wings and lifted her big body into the air. It was going to be a hard flight for her as the wind was very, very strong. "Keep safe!" she called.

"Petersmith you have been amazing but where is your friend Spit?"

"I don't think he is coming McDragon," sobbed the boy. "It seems McMuran is a wizard and he pointed his wand at him and stunned him with fire from it. I think he must be dead as the new scale he gave me has been cold in my hand and I have called and called. Is there time for me to go back and look for him please?"

McDragon had a very sad look on his face as did Haribald.

"Petersmith, the seer's cave did not show any pictures of Spit after the rescue, apart from the one where we saw you both running and if we do not leave immediately we will not be able to get you back to the house for some time. The storm is nearly upon us and it is going to be a bad one. I am so sorry but there is nothing more we can do today. Climb up on me and let's be off."

Haribald nodded in agreement. He would go with them to make sure they could fight off any squawkin attacks. Before joining Seraphina and the Pearl. She was taking a different route to them.

CHAPTER TWENTY TWO

As they lifted up into the racing wind Peter tried to overcome his tremendous grief at losing his two newly found friends and he collapsed in a sodden heap on the back of the dragon. He felt he had failed them but at the same time he was so proud to have known such an amazing young dragon. He couldn't remember feeling so much heartbreak before.

"There, there, Petersmith. Spit was a very brave dragon. He will be remembered by dragons for all time!"

Peter got the small scale out of his pocket, wanting to feel close to Spit even though he knew he was dead. It was still cold in his hand.

They hugged the coast of the small island flying as low as possible to try and keep from being blown off course.

Suddenly Peter cried out, "McDragon please turn around. The scale is warming, something is happening!"

McDragon did an amazing twist in mid-air, one of his wings brushing the cliff face as it did, knocking some seabirds out of their nest. Haribald copied the manoeuvre and they sped back the way they had come.

"Spit, Spit are you there?" Peter shouted.

"I am coming!"

"We are on our way back to get you Spit! Wait by the dome where I go in and out!" He was overjoyed and the tears which had been streaming down his face were immediately replaced by a big beam.

They landed at the top of the slope and Peter ran down it and popped into the dome. The dragons followed but remained outside the barrier. There was lots of smoke inside and Peter coughed and coughed but couldn't see anything. Then out of the gloom he saw a big shape looming towards him. He inched back carefully so that he could feel the slight pressure of the bubbledome wall against him as the dome wall opened a little, and then he stayed put, ensuring that it could not close unless he moved. The two fully grown dragons put their big snouts either side of him and pulled and pulled at the magic doorway so that it widened, just like Seraphina had said it was shown in the dragon seer's sketch.

Spit hobbled towards him and Peter shouted encouragement. At the moment that Spit reached him he leapt out of the way so that the little dragon could burst through the gap, splatting himself against the grassy bank the other side followed closely by Peter. The older dragons let go and the barrier popped shut just as a blast of fire streamed towards them. The fire was safely contained inside the bubble.

"Thank you!" Spit panted.

Peter threw his arms around his neck, "I thought you were dead!"

"So did I!" was the answer but all the time Spit was

staring at the huge dragons either side of Peter. Then he ceremoniously bowed his head to each of them in turn and hummed. They returned the compliment by both giving him a pat on the head with the tips of their noses and humming too.

"Petersmith, we must go now – there will be time for all stories to be told later but firstly I will warm you again."

Haribald did the same to Spit so that he would not feel the cold as they went high in the sky. Once that was done Peter clambered up onto McDragon's back and felt the scales clamp down on his knees to hold him in place. Haribald ordered Spit to do the same. Spit had to use the slope to help him get up high enough to climb on top. Peter could see that Haribald's scales also locked down on Spit's hind legs. Then they were up and off. They looked a very strange sight indeed.

Just as they started to climb up towards the grey swirling clouds there was a loud caw and out of nowhere Archie burst out of the dome towards them. He was looking very, very battered and it was obvious that he was finding it extremely hard to fly against the strong wind.

"Come here Archie and get into my jacket!" yelled Peter. If a crow could look relieved then Archie certainly did as he landed on Peter's arm and Peter tucked him safely inside his jacket. Peter zipped it up, leaving only Archie's head out. He felt happy now that he knew both of his friends were still alive and safely out of the dome, albeit a little worse for wear and he was on his way back to his family. He smiled and made sure his pair of dragon scales were safely stowed away so that if there were any attacks he wouldn't lose them.

In the pocket his fingers felt a soft squidgy mess – it was the remains of the lardy cake. He was very tired but more importantly, he was extremely hungry after such a big adventure. He squeezed some of the cake between his fingers and offered it to Archie, who gobbled it up ravenously. Peter too took an enormous bite of the squashed cake which made his cheeks bulge up and down as he chewed. When they had finished it they both started to nod off despite the gale blowing them about.

A sudden swerving from McDragon jolted Peter awake. Three red squawkins were diving down towards them. McDragon twisted and turned his back on them to slap one of them very hard with his tail. It could be heard screaming its way towards the sea beneath them. Haribald was doing his best to knock the other two out of the way, but they were having none of it. Then Peter looked at Spit sitting akimbo on top of Haribald's back. He looked incredibly strange squatted there and oddly he seemed to be rubbing his mouth on one of his feet. Suddenly, he raised his head and with fierce dragon eyes blew out a stream of fire straight at one squawkin. Peter could smell the singed shell of the squawkin even from where he was. It too plummeted past him screeching loudly. Spit puffed himself up again and whoosh! He aimed fire at the last one which was still attacking Haribald. That sorted it out nicely!

If Spit had been a human he would have brushed his hands together as if to say, there, that got rid of them. Haribald must have said something to the little dragon because Spit seemed to straighten up on the huge dragon's back.

Peter raised his fist and waved at his friend who nodded regally back at him, a big proud dragon grin on his face.

As the high winds battered the dragons, they were pushed from side to side, hither and thither. The waves beneath them were huge and scary surging up and down getting higher and higher. As time passed, the wind dropped slightly and Peter was relieved to see that they were now over land.

The landscape below them looked rocky and green and very familiar.

"Nearly there Petersmith, nearly there!"

As McDragon said this, Haribald suddenly veered off to the right and started to move away from them trumpeting as he did. Spit trumpeted too.

"Where are they going, McDragon?"

"They will be joining Seraphina and the Pearl. Your little friend did an amazing job dealing with those two squawkins. Haribald was having a problem getting rid of them." Peter grinned at the thought of how happy Spit would be now. He had wanted to breathe fire and he had certainly done that today.

"If the storm dies down I will take you and Archie to see him tomorrow Petersmith."

"Oh, thank you McDragon. That would be amazing. Did you hear that Archie? You might be able to see your friend Spit tomorrow?" Archie cave a soft caw. "It's been a tough day today hasn't it?"

"Yes, but we dragons knew that rescuing the Pearl was going to take an enormous amount of our strength and the immense bravery of a small dragon boy." That made the tired boy smile.

The cottage was in sight and McDragon gradually lowered himself downwards to land very gently on top of his rocks.

Peter scrambled down from his perch as soon as the scales released his knees. He kept hold of Archie who was still inside his coat.

McDragon dropped his head down towards the boy and peered at him, his amethyst eyes burning brightly.

"You stood up so well to your task Petersmith. You have overcome all odds in the quest to help save us dragons from dying out and I thank you from the bottom of my big dragon heart!"

Peter felt quite tearful for a moment and then very proud. He straightened up, rather like a soldier.

"Thank you McDragon. I am so pleased we have managed to get the Pearl back for Seraphina and Haribald and that we rescued Spit and Archie. My heart felt like it would break when I thought they were dead. But what about McMuran, do you think he will have survived the fire in the magic bubbledome?"

"I know not whether he will survive or indeed why he wanted a dragon's Pearl. It is a mystery. Now, dragon kin, go home and sleep. I too will slumber until early in the morning."

Peter could see how the big dragon's head was drooping with exhaustion so with a small wave he left him and walked slowly back towards the house. Rain was beginning to fall in earnest soaking his hair.

Lifting Archie out of his jacket he asked, "Where shall we put you Archie so you can rest? I will bring you some food a little later."

Archie spread out his wings, cawed and then flew up into a nearby pine tree. He settled himself down onto a branch and tucked his head under his wing.

Peter trudged on and into the house where his mum had just got the fruit cake out of the oven and it smelt delicious.

"Good old dragon time!" he thought as he walked across to her to put his arms around her waist and bury his head in her chest.

"Oh there you are Peter! You are quite wet! What's this all about? It's not like you at all."

"Well I was thinking today how much I love you and dad and that I never tell you. It was when I was worrying about dad getting back from the island in the storm and it made me think how I take you for granted sometimes."

"Thank you Peter that is one of the nicest things you have ever said to me. Dad and I both love you very much as well. Your dad rang to say he is now on dry land and will be home very soon, so we'll be able to have that early dinner we talked about." She looked down at him and her voice changed, "What on earth have you been doing? You look quite dirty and battered."

"Oh, I just slipped and fell down mum. Sorry I got my clothes so dirty again!"

"That keeps happening to you. Never mind, go and have a quick bath and change into some clean clothes and put these dirty ones straight into the washing machine. Put your jacket in there as well and we'll get them cleaned up and dried in no time at all. It's so nice having all this time to keep on top of things. Would you like to try a piece of this fruit cake?"

"Oh, yes please! You know I am always hungry here."

Once he had eaten and had a drink of milk he remembered to take his dragon scales out of the jacket pockets, also his unused camera, before he put his clothes into the washing machine and then he walked tiredly up the stairs to grab some clean clothes and go into the bathroom to enjoy a soak in some hot water. A strange boy stared back at him in the mirror. A very dirty boy at that.

CHAPTER TWENTY THREE

The rain finally stopped early that evening although the wind battered and blustered around the outside of the house. After dinner Peter managed to get some bread and milk in a small bowl along with some meat scraps left from their dinner, which he'd found at the top of the waste bin. He snuck out to offer them to Archie. The bird was very happy to see him and flew down to accept the treats, then he returned to the branch to sleep again.

Peter also took to his bed early and he fell into a deep sleep as soon as his head touched the pillows. No dreams disturbed him.

A tap tapping at the window woke him early in the morning and when he looked out the window he could see a big black bird with a big black beak looking in at him. There was no sign of any rain, which was a good sign and he opened the window.

"Did McDragon send you to wake me?"

Archie cawed which Peter took to mean yes.

"OK, I'll just get washed and dressed and I'll see you outside in a jiffy."

He felt well rested and was eager to get down to McDragon's rocks. He was amazed to see that his burnt hand showed no sign of any damage. The frillio must have done its job well. He was very excited to think he would be seeing Spit again.

After creeping down the stairs, as usual as he passed the fruit bowl he took an apple saying, "An apple a day keeps the doctor away!"

It was good to wear a clean jacket but he was not so sure it would still be clean when he got home later if he was seeing Spit.

McDragon too looked refreshed as he greeted Peter. "Good morning Petersmith, Dragon boy!" Peter looked very proud when he heard that name.

"Good morning McDragon. Are we going to see Seraphina and Spit this morning?"

"Yes, indeed we are."

"But what about the storm, I thought it might last longer than that?"

"That seemed to be so, but we are lucky it has passed us here. It has left rough seas everywhere but as we are flying that should not affect us."

"Oh good!"

"Let me warm you and then you can hop up."

Peter waited while he was warmed through and then pulled himself into position. The scales snapped down to secure him and before he knew it they were off, flying high in the sky over very rough water with Archie flying alongside them. The waves all had white horses on their crests and the sea was a dark grey colour making the air smell very salty.

"Seraphina has chosen a very secure eerie this time and it will not take long for us to get there. Luckily we are in dragon time so your family will not miss you at all."

Peter lost track of their direction quite quickly but then he noticed that they were beginning to descend towards a very small craggy island. Far too small for anyone to live on it. Down and down they went scaring a lot of seabirds who flew wither and thither squawking loudly. They had been going to and from their nests on the small, but tall, cliff face.

They landed perfectly on some rocks quite high above the seabirds.

"Your landings are so much better now McDragon."

The dragon just hurumphed in response.

Peter skidded down from his perch as soon as the scales had unlocked his knees. Then he heard, rather than saw, a shuffling and jumping sound and there was Spit! He was obviously very excited and was leaping about and swinging his tail from side to side making dust fly about. Peter was very pleased to notice that there were no pine needles or thick dirt, so it was nowhere near as bad as it had been in the magician's dome. It was just a bit dusty.

As Spit rushed towards them he called out, "How do you do, Petersmith?!"

"I'm very well thank you. How do you do Spit? Are you happy to be free of the dome?"

"Oh yes! Thank you Petersmith, thank you so much for coming back for me!"

"I couldn't leave my friend behind!"

Archie cawed and flew about Spit's head and Spit giggled in his dragon way. "How do you do Archie?!

It's so good to see you too!" bellowed the small dragon. McDragon snorted in amusement at the pair.

Then Spit galloped towards McDragon and skidded to a sudden stop. He bowed low to his elder and hummed.

McDragon too bowed his head in response, obviously appreciating the young dragon's greeting and he hummed a reply.

"Come along Petersmith! It's nearly time!"

"Time for what Spit!"

"For the hatching of course! Seraphina has worked some amazing dragon magic and managed to hold it off until you arrived. Hurry up, come on, this way!"

Peter and McDragon followed Spit, Archie flying close by. As they neared a clearing they all stopped. There in the centre of a small circle of rocks were Seraphina and Haribald d'Ness both looking down intently at the grey speckled Pearl. The Pearl was rocking to and fro much faster than when Peter had last seen it and once she saw them, Seraphina dipped her proud head and touched the egg gently with her nose. The rocking stopped immediately and Peter could see that the split which was down its centre was now deepening. It made a loud cracking noise and then broke in two.

"Wow!" was all that Peter could say.

Inside the sac that came out of the egg was a small, but perfectly formed dragon. Seraphina bit the sac and tore it open. The tiny dragon popped out and wobbled about, nearly falling flat on its face but Seraphina nudged it and then snorted heat onto it. The little dragonite snorted back and they touched noses holding in that position for a time. Once contact was broken, the little one staggered right up to her mum. Seraphina let herself down gently on top of it so all but its head was covered by her great big chest. Peter could see the gap over her heart where his scale had been taken. It brought tears to his eyes when he saw how content Seraphina now looked. Haribald stepped cautiously across to his mate who was now humming and he started humming too. Then McDragon joined in the dragon song and Spit, looking a little bemused started to hum as well. It was a lovely sound and Peter wanted very much to hum like a dragon to show his appreciation of the newly hatched dragonite. In the end, despite feeling very embarrassed he hummed along with them – it just felt that it was the right thing to do.

Eventually once the dragon song had finished Seraphina stood up and walked slowly across to stand in front of Peter. The dragonite followed her on unsteady legs showing that she knew who her mum was.

"Petersmith, we dragons owe you a great debt! Without you this little dragon would have been bonded to that wizard. What's more, Spit would still be imprisoned in the magical dome. It would mean a great deal to me and Haribald if you would now name our little one, who is very special to us all. As I told you before, she is a female dragon so when she is older she will join with another dragon and that will ensure that dragons survive. Furthermore, now that I am released from my oath I will also produce at least one other if not more Pearls. What say you Petersmith – what name would you like to give her?"

Peter just stood there with his mouth open – he was to name a dragon!!! In his wildest dreams he had never done that!

"Ooer! I am very honoured Seraphina and Haribald d'Ness." He answered, giving Haribald his full title and dipping his head towards them both at the same time.

Even Spit looked solemn.

Peter thought hard and wrinkled up his nose while he looked at the little thing which was now hopping and popping around her mother dragon. She was already much steadier on her feet even though she had hatched such a short time ago. She stretched out her tiny wings and gave them a small wave, nearly toppling over when they unbalanced her.

"Popsicle! Popple for short!" he announced, "as she is popping about."

The dragons hummed in unison again and Popple looked like she was humming as well. It seemed she liked her name.

As Peter watched her proudly, something caught his attention out of the corner of his eye. Something very bright.

"Oh, another frillio!"

"Not quite Petersmith," answered Spit, "it's actually the same frillio that was in the magic bubbledome." And he walked over and pushed his snout down into the frillio and when he pulled it out his nose was very pink.

"Mmmmmm!"

"How did it get here Spit?"

"Well, when I was rushing away from the flames trying to catch you up, I passed by her, I call her a she because of her pretty colour. I thought the flames would devour her so I scooped her up in my mouth and brought her with me."

"So that is what you were fiddling about with when the squawkins attacked us?"

"Indeed Petersmith, I was moving her so she was not in my mouth anymore."

"Oh Spit, you are amazing! But will she live?"

"She is not a plant but a living being of some kind. If you look at her you will notice she is a very bright pink now so she must be happy after her travels. Why don't you touch her?"

Peter put his right hand into the centre of the beautiful frillio and felt that same wonderful comforting softness as he had before.

"Yes, Spit, I think you are right."

"Petersmith!" McDragon called to him, "it will not be too long before we must leave so let us talk awhile."

Peter returned to the three dragons with Spit trailing along behind him. He settled himself down on a nearby rock so he could watch Popple at the same time.

"I was wondering, McDragon, do you believe that Spit may be something to do with Arletta, whose skeleton was in the dome?"

Spit had started his dancing about again and was raising dust clouds around him.

"Spit! Please can you stop that, it makes me cough!"

Spit looked a little bit shamefaced and just tried to jiggle about without moving his tail.

"Petersmith, it is exciting to think that the dragon bones of Arletta could be those of one of my relatives. Sad as well, of course," he added quickly.

"That thought had crossed my mind Petersmith, but we will not know for sure until Spit can go to see what the dragon seer's pictures show. Until that time he will stay here and learn from Seraphina and Haribald. He has much to catch up on as he has not been with another dragon before now." Answered McDragon. "Also, the other strangeness is that we do not know how it came about that Spit did not bond with McMuran, which would have happened if he had been nearby when Spit's Pearl opened."

"And what about McMuran, do you dragons believe he is a descendant of one of the original magicians, maybe, what was his name, Murani?"

"It is quite likely Petersmith. It is also quite possible that he has survived that fire in the dome, after all he is a wizard. Let's hope he does not try and take any more dragons or Pearls or we may have to call upon our dragon kin, Petersmith, again."

Peter grinned proudly.

"Petersmith!" this came from Seraphina. "We will always welcome you into our midst. Remember to use my scale at any time and I will answer."

* * *

Spit and Peter spent the rest of the short time Peter was on the island happily playing with one another. Spit was so full of beans that Peter felt quite bruised when it was finally time for him to get back to the cottage. Fortunately, he'd had the forethought to take off his jacket while they messed about. McDragon promised to bring him again for the last couple of mornings of his holiday. Sadly, it was nearly time for him to return to his other, not so exciting, life.

CHAPTER TWENTY FOUR

In the car going home Peter was feeling very low indeed. He was not sure when he would be able to see Spit again or Popple for that matter. In the couple of days that McDragon had taken him to the island she had already changed. She'd taken to tagging along behind Spit and Peter when they were playing and they often had to hold back on their games to make sure they didn't hurt her. For all that she was a very tough tiny thing and Peter had grown very fond of her.

McDragon and Seraphina had agreed that any time Peter was in Scotland, one of them would come and transport him to the island for a visit using dragon time. He knew he could use the scales to keep up to date with them all. They all hoped that it would not be too long before Spit could also fly, but each dragon was different and Spit had not had the luxury of being in the open air and strengthening his wings every day.

Now Peter was looking forward to the pleasure of facing Biffy and his gang again. Spit had told him he was silly to dread that, after all, he had taken on a magician and that horrible thing, Slider and without him the dragons would not have been saved. They would forever be in his debt.

McDragon had just nodded sagely to Peter and all he would say was, "You will see Petersmith, all will be well. You are dragon kin!" Which really didn't help him at all.

On his last morning with them, all four dragons and the tiny Popple surrounded him and hummed their dragon song at him. It made him feel so proud and content to hear them. No-one else in the world would have had dragons sing to them and it was a very emotional moment. The humming made him feel as if the world was a good place to be and that feeling stayed with him all the way back to the cottage, even helping through his parting with McDragon who had touched him on the forehead with his enormous snout, leaving him a burning spot on his head.

It was egg sandwiches again in the car and the smell was quite strong. At least this time they were not squashed and they managed to make the whole journey without Alice being sick. It was a very long journey but Peter spent it thinking of his dragon family and occasionally touching Spit's scale so he could see what he was doing. Popple was often with him so Peter could watch her as well.

"Dad?"

"Yes, son?"

"Do you need to go to Scotland again sometime soon?" he asked hopefully.

"Quite possibly. I actually left something at Mr McMuran's house which if he doesn't post it to me I will need to pick up next time I am there. I can manage without it for now but he hasn't been answering his telephone so I wonder if he has gone away for a little while. I have other places to write about as well. Why do you ask Peter?"

"I loved Scotland dad, and I would really, really like to go back if you do!"

His mum, who was doing the driving at the time responded to him, "I'm so glad you had a good time Peter, particularly as you didn't want to go there in the first place. We would all like to go back again if dad can take us, so perhaps he could arrange his trip in the next holidays."

Peter felt better knowing there was something to look forward to because he had so many unanswered questions about the dragons.

* * *

The start of school loomed over him and the last few days of the holiday were filled with shopping for new uniforms and books. The closer it got the more Peter worried and he struggled to sleep some nights. In his mind's eye he could picture Biffy terrorising him and he made such a big thing of it that he imagined Biffy doing far worse things to him than he ever had in the past.

School started a little later on the first day back and he dressed reluctantly in his new clothes hoping they would stay intact. With his heart in his mouth he dragged his heels all the way to the school gates. Just before he reached them he felt in his pocket for Spit's scale and made brief contact with him so that he would have something happy to think on.

"Be brave Petersmith! You are dragon kin!" Peter could see Popple was nearby and the sun was shining in their little place, a rainbow coloured the sky behind them.

Peter kept hold of the scale just to give him a little bit of confidence as he stepped onto the school grounds. Immediately he heard that horrible voice, "Ah, the crip! We've been waiting for you Dragon boy!" He found himself surrounded by the gang who were jostling him from side to side. It was very hard to stay upright.

He braced himself and tried to remember all that he had achieved in Scotland and the friends he had made there.

A small dragon giggle seemed to vibrate through him and, as Peter drew in a breath, there was a loud bang and Biffy and his cronies were suddenly all flat on their backs! Peter was standing in the centre of them and there was the smell of singed hair and smoke – it was almost as if a firework had gone off near them and knocked them all down. The dragon giggle became louder and louder and Peter realised that Spit was laughing and rolling about.

"I told you that you are dragon kin Petersmith!!"

Peter carried on walking towards his classroom. Looking back over his shoulder he could see Biffy and the bullies struggling to their feet and looking bewilderedly at each other as if to ask what had happened!

"You are quite correct Spit, I am definitely dragon kin! Thank you. Speak to you later. Over and Out!!"

"Over and Out Petersmith!"

If you enjoyed reading about Peter and the dragons of Scotland and their fight with the wizard, McMuran, then please follow me on my Facebook page: Pam G Howard@ Pamghowardchildrensbooks or Twitter: Pam Howard@ Pamghoward.

I hope to publish Book Two of the McDragon series later in 2017. You can read a taster of it on the next page.

Why not also try the first book in my other series, "Spangle" which is about a young girl who has to escape from her wicked aunt to try and find her family. She is helped in her quest by the magical, Mr Spangle, and various ghosts. This is available from Amazon.

Effel
The second book in the McDragon series

CHAPTER ONE

The rope tightened and the dragon roared in frustration snorting angrily out of his nostrils – he couldn't move – he was trapped. He knew he was going to need the help of the young boy Petersmith, again because he was the honey in the trap and if the other dragons tried to rescue him they would also be caught.

* * *

It was raining heavily on the tent, it was a soothing sound and what's more for a short time Peter had the space to himself. A school camping trip to Scotland was not his idea of fun at all, there were seven of them sleeping in the tent and it felt overcrowded.

Now where on earth was Spit's dragon scale, he needed to use it to talk to the little dragon before anyone came back. The last message he had had from Spit was that there was something badly wrong – McDragon was missing. He had not been for his daily visit for a few days. Peter desperately wanted to know if there was any news at all but he needed his dragon friend's scale to do that. On his recent visit to the Isle of Harris, the young dragon Spit, had given him a scale from his chest so that they could use it to talk to one another. He had another dragon scale, which the adult dragon, Seraphina, had given him for the same purpose, but it was hidden at home for safe keeping while he was away.

He was positive that he had secreted the scale under the soap in his soap box and that had been inside his washing kit but it wasn't there! He tipped the whole bag out carefully on the top of his camp bed and went through each item individually. Nothing. The only reason he had put it there was that he'd had to go out for the rafting trip on the loch and he didn't want to take any chances of losing it in the water.

He was beginning to panic!

Was McDragon alright? He really needed to know!

Now where on earth was that scale!

After searching thoroughly yet again he realised it was definitely missing, which was a disaster.

A head poked through the tent flap, "Peter, you need to come out for supper now!"

"I'll be right with you," he replied starting to carefully put everything back into the wash bag and checking it all over yet again as he did. He took another look over the sleeping bag and then inside it, in case it had fallen out unnoticed. Eventually he woefully had to give up before someone else came along to insist he came out for dinner.

Dinner today was cottage pie and baked beans which was quite filling and tasty and then there was a pudding. Each tent had to take turns at cooking, fortunately his tent's team had done their shift yesterday so they had tonight off.

* * *

The next day's role call was bright and early and the sun was beginning to shine through some misty light rain so a beautiful rainbow lit up some of the sky.

Peter thought to himself, "There is often a crock of gold at the end of a rainbow so where does that one end?" and he pinpointed where he thought it should be. Strangely the end of it seemed to move over to the left a tad as he stared at it.

"I'll go there when we have our break and investigate," he thought.

Then he remembered the lost dragon scale. There really wasn't much he could do about it as he could hardly ask anyone if they'd seen it – they would have mocked him for the rest of the trip. They weren't to know of his adventures with the dragons in Scotland during the summer holidays where he had met his best friend Spit the dragon, when they rescued Seraphina's Pearl, the dragons' name for a dragon egg, which had led to him now being counted as dragon kin.

As he looked up he saw Biffy staring oddly at something in his hand, glancing over at Peter with a very strange look on his face. As soon as he saw Peter watching him he turned away quickly and walked off.

"That was odd!" Peter muttered to himself. "Could he have....? Ridiculous! Of course not!" He answered his unfinished question. But as he pondered further over this he realised that Biffy had been one of the few people who had been let off the rafting trip.

Biffy and his cronies used to torment him and call him the Crip because his left hand only had a thumb and two fingers on it. Spit had put an end to their bullying by magically blasting them when Peter was holding on to his dragon scale and the boys had all fallen down around him looking dazed and smelling rather singed. Biffy's only name for him now was "Dragon boy" and that was because one silly day he had been day dreaming in class and answered the teacher's question by saying something about dragons. He had never heard the end of that one!

* * *